ONCE MISSED

TAKING (Book #4)
STALKING (Book #5)

RILEY PAIGE MYSTERY SERIES
ONCE GONE (Book #1)
ONCE TAKEN (Book #2)
ONCE CRAVED (Book #3)
ONCE LURED (Book #4)
ONCE HUNTED (Book #5)
ONCE PINED (Book #6)
ONCE FORSAKEN (Book #7)
ONCE COLD (Book #8)
ONCE STALKED (Book #9)
ONCE LOST (Book #10)
ONCE BURIED (Book #11)
ONCE BOUND (Book #12)
ONCE TRAPPED (Book #13)
ONCE DORMANT (Book #14)
ONCE SHUNNED (Book #15)
ONCE MISSED (Book #16)

MACKENZIE WHITE MYSTERY SERIES
BEFORE HE KILLS (Book #1)
BEFORE HE SEES (Book #2)
BEFORE HE COVETS (Book #3)
BEFORE HE TAKES (Book #4)
BEFORE HE NEEDS (Book #5)
BEFORE HE FEELS (Book #6)
BEFORE HE SINS (Book #7)
BEFORE HE HUNTS (Book #8)
BEFORE HE PREYS (Book #9)
BEFORE HE LONGS (Book #10)
BEFORE HE LAPSES (Book #11)
BEFORE HE ENVIES (Book #12)
BEFORE HE STALKS (Book #13)

ONCE MISSED

A Riley Paige Mystery—Book 16

BLAKE PIERCE

BLAKE PIERCE

Blake Pierce is author of the bestselling RILEY PAGE mystery series, which includes fifteen books (and counting). Blake Pierce is also the author of the MACKENZIE WHITE mystery series, comprising thirteen books (and counting); of the AVERY BLACK mystery series, comprising six books; of the KERI LOCKE mystery series, comprising five books; of the MAKING OF RILEY PAIGE mystery series, comprising five books (and counting); of the KATE WISE mystery series, comprising six books (and counting); of the CHLOE FINE psychological suspense mystery, comprising six books (and counting); and of the JESSE HUNT psychological suspense thriller series, comprising five books (and counting).

ONCE GONE (a Riley Paige Mystery—Book #1), BEFORE HE KILLS (A Mackenzie White Mystery—Book 1), CAUSE TO KILL (An Avery Black Mystery—Book 1), A TRACE OF DEATH (A Keri Locke Mystery—Book 1), and WATCHING (The Making of Riley Paige—Book 1) are each available as a free download on Amazon!

An avid reader and lifelong fan of the mystery and thriller genres, Blake loves to hear from you, so please feel free to visit www.blakepierceauthor.com to learn more and stay in touch.

TABLE OF CONTENTS

PROLOGUE

Lori Tovar pulled her car into the driveway of the house where she'd lived for most of her life. She stopped the engine and just sat there staring at the charming three-story dwelling.

A familiar phrase went through her mind.

First to arrive, last to leave.

She smiled a bit sadly. She'd heard people say that a lot about her.

Working as a nurse at South Hill Hospital, she was known to take longer shifts than anyone else. She often filled in for other nurses' absences while seldom taking any time off for herself. It wasn't that she felt especially diligent. It was just that, somehow, working long hours came kind of naturally to her.

She murmured those words aloud, "First to arrive, last to leave."

The phrase was the story of her life in more ways than one. She'd been the firstborn child out of four to live in this big, once-happy house. During the last few years, her younger siblings had spread out all over the country.

And of course, Dad had simply gone away. Nobody had seen that coming.

Lori and her brothers and sister had always felt as though they'd belonged to a picture-perfect family. It had come as a shock to all of them to find out otherwise a couple of years ago, when Dad had left Mom for another woman.

And now, here Lori was—the last child left in town, so always the one who came around to check in on Mom. She'd stop by at least once a week, maybe take her out for coffee, or just sit with her and talk and do her best to cheer her mother out of spells of deep sadness.

Last to leave.

Lori heaved a long sigh, then got out of the car and walked past the immaculate terraced plants and shrubbery toward the front porch. She stopped at the mailbox and opened it to see if there was any mail. The box was empty.

Lori figured Mom must have already checked it, which might be a good sign. Maybe it meant that Mom wasn't slipping into one of her bouts of extreme apathy.

But Lori was dismayed that the door swung open when she turned the knob. She shook her head. She must have told Mom a thousand times that she needed to keep the door locked, even during the day, especially now that she was living alone.

During Lori's childhood and teenage years, locking the door all the time hadn't been necessary. But those had been more innocent times. Things had changed, and crime was up even in this well-to-do neighborhood. Break-ins were getting more and more common.

Guess I'll have to remind her again, Lori thought.

Not that it would do any good.

Old habits die hard.

She stepped into the house and called out, "Mom, I got off work early. Just thought I'd stop by."

No answer came.

She called out again, "Mom, are you home?"

Again there was no answer. Lori wasn't especially surprised. Mom might be napping upstairs. This wouldn't be the first time she hadn't heard Lori arrive because she was asleep.

But it wasn't good that Mom had left the door unlocked while she was napping.

I'll have to talk to her about that.

Meanwhile, Lori felt a bit undecided. It seemed a shame to go upstairs and wake Mom up if she was sleeping soundly. On the other hand, she'd gone to a certain amount of trouble arranging her work schedule in order to stop by.

I should have called first, she told herself.

2

She decided she'd go upstairs and peek in her parents' bedroom and try to see just how soundly Mom was sleeping. If she was starting to wake up, Lori would let her know she was here. Otherwise, maybe she'd just leave quietly.

As she headed up the stairs, Lori was seized by a familiar spell of deep nostalgia. As always, this house was haunted by memories, most of them very pleasant. There was nothing really wrong with Lori's life now, but she couldn't help but think that she'd spent her happiest days right here.

Will I ever be that happy again? she wondered.

She hoped someday her life would be a little more complete than it was right now.

And wouldn't it be wonderful if that could happen right here?

Lori and her husband, Roy, often talked about buying this house. They both thought that Mom would be better off in a smaller home, maybe a cozy apartment that she could easily take care of, and where she wasn't constantly reminded of how Dad had left her. Certainly it would be better for her general mood.

Lori thought that this would be a perfect place to start her own family, which she and Roy both figured ought to be soon. For a moment she thought she could almost hear the sound of children laughing, running from bedroom to bedroom as she and her siblings had years ago. If only Mom would agree to move, and of course to give them a financial deal that they could manage.

Mom often said that she was getting impatient to have grandchildren, but she didn't seem to realize that moving out could speed up that process. She stubbornly insisted on staying right here, refusing to think of living anywhere else.

Maybe someday she'll change her mind, Lori thought.

If so, she wished it happened before she started having children,

When Lori stepped into the second-story hallway, she noticed that the door to Mom's bedroom was partially open. Mom usually closed it whenever she took a nap. Suddenly it seemed a little strange that Mom hadn't heard her call out from downstairs. Was she maybe getting a little hard of hearing? If so, Lori hadn't noticed it.

Lori walked to the bedroom door and silently pushed it the rest of the way open. Nobody was in the bedroom, and the bed was perfectly made.

She figured Mom must have gone out somewhere.

And that's probably a good thing.

Mom had been spending too much time shut up alone inside this enormous house. When Lori had visited a few days ago, Mom had mentioned maybe going out with some of the friends she played bingo with on Fridays at the church. Lori had told her that she thought that would be an excellent idea.

But this wasn't Friday, and wherever Mom had gone, it was troubling that she'd left the front door unlocked. Lori wondered—was Mom maybe mentally slipping a little? The thought had worried her lately. Mom's memory had always been exceptionally sharp, but she had been forgetting little things lately.

Lori tried to assure herself that Mom was still pretty young for dementia to be setting in. But from her own work at the hospital, she knew it was a possibility. She hated the thought of having to talk to Mom about that, and also all the troubles and heartache that would surely ensue.

Meanwhile, Lori decided she might as well head on home.

She walked back down the stairs and paused to glance over into the dining room. She felt a pang at not seeing the long dining room table where she and her sister and brothers had enjoyed delicious dinners and conversations with Mom and Dad.

As determined as Mom was to live much as she always had, she just hadn't been able to sit at that big table anymore. It had had plenty of room for all the family members who were no longer here, and it could even be expanded for company by adding extra leaves. Lori could understand why Mom had wanted the table gone. Lori had helped sell it and its matching chairs, and they'd bought a smaller dining room set.

Then Lori noticed something odd. There were usually four chairs around that new square table. But there were only three chairs there now.

Mom must have moved the missing chair, but why?

Maybe she'd used it to reach a shelf or change a light bulb.

Lori frowned as she thought, *Another thing I've got to talk to her about.*

Mom had a perfectly good stepladder, after all, which was much safer for tasks of that sort. She ought to know better than to use a chair.

As Lori glanced around looking for some sign of the chair, her eyes fell on the narrow marble counter that separated the dining room from the kitchen. She saw a reddish splotch on the far side.

That was truly odd. Mom was always a meticulous housekeeper who was especially obsessed with keeping her kitchen clean. It wasn't like her to spill something and not clean it up immediately.

Lori felt a tingle of mounting worry.

Something is wrong, she thought.

She hurried to the edge of the counter and looked into the kitchen.

There on the floor lay her mother, splayed awkwardly in a pool of blood.

"Mom!" she gasped in a hoarse voice.

Her heart was pounding, and she felt her arms and legs grow cold and numb. She knew she was going into shock, but she had to keep her wits together.

Lori knelt down and saw that her mother's eyes were closed. There was a large gash on her head. Lori felt herself grappling with disbelief, horror, and confusion, and her mind raced as she tried to grasp…

What happened?

Mom must have stumbled and fallen and hit her head against the countertop.

Her medical reflexes kicking in, Lori reached to touch Mom's neck to check her pulse.

And that's when Lori saw Mom's throat had been slashed.

One carotid artery had been severed, but there was no blood pulsing out of it.

Her mother's face was pale and utterly lifeless.

Lori felt a volcanic force erupt from deep in her lungs.

Then she began to scream.

CHAPTER ONE

A shot rang out from somewhere very close by.

Riley Paige whirled around as the noise resonated through her upstairs hallway.

April! she thought, as shock charged through her body.

Riley dashed to her bedroom.

Her sixteen-year-old daughter April was standing there shaking from head to foot, but she didn't seem to be wounded.

Riley could breathe again.

On the floor in front of April lay a Ruger SR22 pistol. Next to it was the blue vinyl box the gun was supposed to be kept in.

April's voice quavered as she said, "I'm sorry. I was getting ready to put it in the safe in the closet, and it went off and I dropped it. I didn't know it was loaded."

Riley felt her face flush. Her fear was turning into anger.

"What do you mean, you didn't know?" she said. "How could you not know?"

Riley picked up the gun and popped out the magazine and waved it at April.

"This magazine shouldn't even be in the gun," she said. "You were supposed to take it out before we left the shooting range."

"I thought I'd fired all the rounds," April said.

"That's no excuse," Riley snapped. "You *always* remove the magazine when you finish target practice."

"I know," April said. "It won't happen again."

Damn right it won't happen again, Riley thought. She realized she was also angry with herself for stepping out of the room before April had put the gun away. But they had already put in several sessions at the practice range, and everything had gone smoothly before.

She glanced around the room.

"Where did it hit?" she asked.

April pointed toward the back wall. Sure enough, Riley saw a bullet hole. She felt a renewed wave of panic. She knew that the walls between the rooms inside her house weren't solid enough to stop a bullet—not even from a .22 pistol.

She wagged her finger at April and said, "You stay right here."

She went out into the hall and stepped inside the adjoining room, which was April's bedroom. There was an exit hole in the wall right where she'd expected to see it, then another hole in the opposite wall where the bullet had kept on going.

Riley struggled to clear her head to assess the situation.

Beyond that wall was the backyard.

Could it have hit anybody? she wondered.

She walked over to the hole and peered into it. If the bullet had continued on through, she ought to have been able to see sunlight. The brick exterior must have finally stopped it. And even if it hadn't, the bullet would have been slowed enough not to get beyond the backyard.

Riley exhaled with relief.

No one was hurt.

Even so, this was an awful thing to have happened.

As she left April's bedroom and headed back to her own room, two people reached the top of the stairs and charged into the hallway. One was her fourteen-year-old daughter, Jilly. The other was her stout Guatemalan housekeeper, Gabriela.

Gabriela cried out, "*¡Dios mio!* What was that noise?"

"What happened?" Jilly echoed. "Where's April?"

Before Riley could even begin trying to explain, Jilly and Gabriela had located April in the bedroom. Riley followed after them.

As they all entered, April was putting the vinyl box into the little black safe on the closet shelf. With an obvious effort to appear calm, she said, "My gun went off."

Almost in unison, Jilly and Gabriela exclaimed, "You've got a gun?"

Riley couldn't hold back a groan of despair. The situation was now bad on all sorts of new levels. When Riley had bought the gun for April back in June, they had both agreed not to mention it to either Gabriela or Jilly. Jilly would surely have been jealous of her older sister. Gabriela would simply have worried.

With good reason, as things turned out, Riley thought.

She could see that her youngest daughter was gearing up for an outburst of questions and accusations, while her housekeeper was simply waiting for an explanation.

Riley said, "I'll come downstairs and explain everything to both of you in just a few minutes. Right now I've got to talk to April alone."

Jilly and Gabriela nodded dumbly and left the room. Riley shut the door behind them.

As April plopped down on the bed and looked up at her mother, Riley was reminded how much she and her daughter resembled each other. Even though she was forty-one and April was just sixteen, they were obviously cut from the same cloth. It wasn't just their dark hair and hazel eyes, they also shared an impetuous approach toward life.

Then the teenager slouched over and seemed on the verge of tears. Riley sat down beside her.

"I'm sorry," April said.

Riley didn't reply. An apology just wasn't going to be enough right now.

April said, "Did I do something illegal? Discharging a weapon indoors, I mean? Do we need to notify the police?"

Riley sighed and said, "It's not illegal, no—not if it's accidental. I'm not sure it shouldn't be illegal, though. It was unbelievably careless. Honestly, April, I thought I could trust you with this by now."

April swallowed down a sob and said, "I'm in some pretty serious trouble, aren't I?"

Again, Riley said nothing.

Then April said, "Look, I promise I'll be more careful. It won't happen again. The next time we go to the range—"

Riley shook her head and said, "There won't be a next time."

April's eyes widened.

"You mean …?" she began.

"You can't keep the gun," Riley said. "This is all over."

"But it was just one mistake," April said, her voice getting more shrill.

Riley said, "You know perfectly well that this is a zero-tolerance issue. We've talked about this. Even one stupid, careless mistake like that is one too many. This is very serious, April. Somebody could have gotten hurt or killed. Don't you understand that?"

"But nobody *did* get hurt."

Riley felt stymied. April was moving into full-throttle teenager mode, refusing to accept the reality of what had just happened. Riley knew it was just about impossible to reason with her daughter at times like this. But reasonable or not, this decision was solely Riley's responsibility. In fact, she was the legal owner of the weapon, not April. Her daughter couldn't own a gun until she was eighteen years old.

Riley had bought it because April had said she wanted to become an FBI agent. She'd thought the smaller caliber would make it a good weapon for April to practice with at the gun store's firing range. Until today, those lessons had been going just fine.

April said, "This is kind of your fault, you know. You should have been watching me better."

Riley felt stung. Was April right?

When her daughter had been putting the gun back in its case at the range, Riley had been finishing up her own target practice in the next booth with her own .40 caliber Glock. She'd watched over April plenty of times before. This time she'd thought she could be less vigilant with her.

Obviously she'd been wrong. In spite of all their practice sessions, April still needed close supervision.

No excuses, Riley knew. *No excuses for either of us.*

But that didn't matter. She couldn't let April change her mind by putting her on a guilt trip. Her daughter's next mistake could be deadly.

Riley snapped, "That's not an excuse, and you know it. Putting the gun away properly was your responsibility"

April said miserably, "So you're taking it away from me."

"That's right," Riley said.

"What are you going to do with it?"

"I'm not sure yet," Riley said. She thought she'd probably turn it over to the FBI Academy. They could make it available as a training weapon for new recruits. Meanwhile, she would make sure that it was locked securely in the closet safe.

In a sullen voice, April said, "Well, it's fine with me. I'd changed my mind about wanting to be an FBI agent. I'd been meaning to tell you."

Riley felt an odd jolt at those words.

She knew that April was trying again to make her feel guilty, or at least disappointed.

Instead she felt relieved. She hoped it was true that April was no longer interested in the FBI. Then she wouldn't have to spend years and years worrying for April's life.

"That's your decision to make," Riley said.

"I'll go to my room," her daughter replied.

Without another word, April walked out of the bedroom and shut the door, leaving Riley sitting alone on the bed.

For a moment, she considered following after April, but…

What else is there to say?

Right now, there was nothing. Rationally, Riley knew that she had taken the correct course of action just now. April couldn't be trusted with the gun again. Further scolding and punishment would surely be pointless.

Nevertheless, Riley felt like she'd failed somehow. She wasn't sure why. Maybe, she thought, it was in trusting April to take care of a gun to begin with. But, she wondered, wasn't that part of being a parent? Sooner or later, kids had to be given more responsibilities. They'd fail at some, and they'd succeed at others.

That's just part of growing up.

Surely no parent could predict all of a child's lapses and failures in advance.

Trust was always a risk.

Even so, Riley felt as though her brain was spinning its wheels, trying to generate rationalizations for her own parental failure.

A sudden twinge of pain in her back stopped her ruminations.

My wound.

Her back still hurt from time to time where a psychopathic killer had stabbed her with an icepick. The pick had gone alarmingly deep—deeper than an ordinary knife would likely have gone. It had been just over two weeks ago, and she'd spent a night in the hospital because of it. Then she'd been ordered to remain inactive at home.

Although Riley had been both physically and emotionally shaken by the ordeal, she'd hoped to be back on the job by now, working on a new case. But her boss, Division Chief Brent Meredith, had insisted that she take more time to recover than she'd have liked. He'd put Riley's partner Bill on a leave of absence as well, because he had shot and killed the man who'd stabbed Riley.

She certainly felt ready to get back to work now. She didn't figure a twinge of pain every now and then would interfere with her work. Even though the kids and Gabriela had been waiting on her constantly, she hadn't felt like she'd been connecting well with them. Their constant worry just made her feel guilty and inadequate as a parent.

She knew that right now she had some explaining to do to both Jilly and Gabriela about the gun.

She got up and walked down the hall toward Jilly's room.

Her conversation with Jilly was about as difficult as Riley had expected. Her younger daughter had dark eyes from what had probably been an Italian family heritage and a feisty temper from a difficult early life before Riley had adopted her.

Jilly was openly resentful that Riley had gotten April a gun, and that her sister had been getting target practice behind her back. Of course, Riley couldn't begin to convince her younger daughter that a gun would be out of the question at her age. And besides, it hadn't worked out well for April anyway.

Riley saw that nothing she said was working and she soon gave up.

"Later," she told Jilly. "We'll talk about this again later."

When Riley stepped out of Jilly's doorway, she heard the door close behind her. For a long moment, Riley just stood there in the hallway. Both of her daughters were closed up in their rooms, sulking. Then she sighed and went down the two flights of stairs to Gabriela's living quarters.

Gabriela was sitting on her sofa, gazing out the big glass sliding doors into the backyard. When Riley came in, Gabriela smiled and patted the seat beside her. Riley sat down and began at the beginning, explaining about the gun.

Gabriela didn't get angry—but she did seem to be hurt.

"You should have told me," she said. "You should have trusted me."

"I know," Riley said. "I'm sorry. I guess I'm just...having some trouble in the parenting department these days."

Gabriela shook her head and said, "You try to do too much, *Señora* Riley. There is no such thing as a perfect parent."

Riley's heart warmed at those words.

That's what I needed to hear, she thought.

Gabriela continued, "You should trust me more. You should depend on me more. I am here to make your life easier, after all. That is my job. I am here also to do my share of the parenting. I think I am good with the girls."

"Oh, you are," Riley said, her voice choking a little. "You really are. You have no idea how grateful I am to have you in our lives."

Riley and Gabriela sat smiling at each other in silence for a moment. Riley suddenly felt much, much better.

Then the doorbell rang. Riley gave her housekeeper a big hug and went up to the main floor to answer the door.

For an instant, Riley was delighted to see that her handsome boyfriend, Blaine, had just arrived. But she noticed something wistful about his smile, a melancholy look in his eyes.

This isn't going to be a pleasant visit, she realized.

CHAPTER TWO

Something wasn't right, Riley knew. Instead of walking right in and making himself at home as he usually did, Blaine just stood there outside her front door. He had a vaguely expectant expression on his pleasant features.

Riley's heart sank. She had a pretty good idea what was on Blaine's mind. In fact, she'd been expecting it for days. For a moment she felt an urge to close the door and pretend that he hadn't dropped by right now.

"Come on in," she said.

"Thanks," Blaine replied, and he stepped into the house.

As they sat down in the living room, Riley asked, "Would you like a drink?"

"Uh, no, I don't think so. Thanks."

He doesn't expect this to be a long visit, Riley thought.

Then he looked around and remarked, "The house is awfully quiet. Are the girls out someplace this afternoon?"

Riley almost blurted, *"No, they just don't want to have anything to do with me."*

But that didn't seem right under the circumstances. If things were normal between them, Riley would feel free to vent about the trials of parenthood, and she could expect Blaine to cheerfully commiserate and even lift her spirits with some words of encouragement.

This just wasn't one of those times.

"How are you feeling?" Blaine asked.

For a second it seemed like an odd question, and Riley felt like saying, *"Pretty apprehensive. How about you?"*

But then she realized he was talking about the icepick wound. He'd been extremely attentive and kind to her during her recovery. On many evenings he'd brought over delicious meals from the fine restaurant he owned and managed.

But his very attentiveness had clued her in that something unpleasant was coming. He was always a kind and considerate man, of course. But during the last week or so, there had been a telltale sadness about his kindness—with maybe the hint of an unspoken and unexplained apology.

She said, "I'm feeling much better, thanks."

Blaine nodded, then said slowly and deliberately, "So I guess you'll be going back to work soon."

Here it comes, Riley thought.

"I don't know," she said. "It's up to my boss. He hasn't assigned me to a new case yet."

Blaine squinted at her and said, "But do you feel *ready* to go back to work?"

Riley sighed. She remembered the conversation they'd had shortly after she'd gotten home from the hospital. She'd told him she expected to be able to get back to work in about a week, and he hadn't tried to hide his anxiety at hearing her say that. But they hadn't tried to work things out at the time.

Instead, Riley had squeezed his hand and said, *"I guess we've got some things we need to talk about."*

It had been well over a week since then.

This conversation is overdue, she thought.

She said, "Blaine, I've felt ready to get back to work for days now. I'm more than ready. I'm sorry. I know it's not what you want to hear."

Blaine stared at the floor for a moment.

"Riley, don't you ever think about...?"

His voice faded away.

"About what?" Riley asked, trying to keep a note of bitterness out of her voice. "Getting into a different line of work?"

"I don't know," Blaine said with a shrug. "Surely there are things you can do with the Bureau that don't involve such...risk. You've been a field agent for—what?—nearly twenty years? I know you've been great at it, and I can't tell you how much I admire your dedication and courage. But haven't you given enough of that kind of service? Don't you think you deserve something more?"

He stopped speaking again.

Riley said, "More—safe, you mean? Less dangerous?"

Blaine nodded.

Riley didn't know what to say. Certainly there were choices she could make, even in the BAU. But they would mean huge changes. She couldn't imagine working in the office, just poking through evidence that other agents risked their lives bringing in. Even though she had enjoyed giving occasional lectures at the Academy, she thought it would be hard to teach full time. Describing cases to recruits would only remind her of what she was no longer doing. She couldn't imagine a life of not confronting evil face to face, despite all its dangers.

It would mean abandoning everything she was really good at.

But how could she explain that to Blaine?

Then Blaine said, "I hope you understand—it's not *me* I'm worried about."

Riley felt a sharp stab of understanding.

"I know," she said.

Indeed, she did know that he was perfectly sincere. And that said a lot about Blaine. Riley's work had brought danger into his own life, and he had dealt with it courageously. Last December, a criminal bent on revenge against Riley had come to her house when she wasn't here and tried to kill April and Gabriela. Blaine had come to their rescue, but he had gotten badly injured himself. Riley was still shaken by horror whenever she thought about that ordeal.

Blaine added, "I'm not even worried about *you*, or at least not mostly about you."

"I know," Riley said again.

He didn't have to explain. She knew he was worried about their children—Riley's two daughters and his own teenage daughter, Crystal.

17

And she knew that he had every reason to worry.

Try as she might, she couldn't guarantee their safety as long as she kept living the life she lived. In fact, the safety of everyone around her was already at risk because of criminals she'd encountered, even those she'd beaten. More than once, figures from the past had returned to try for revenge.

Blaine opened his mouth as if searching for the right words to say.

Instead, Riley said, "Blaine, I understand. We don't need to have this talk. We've been having it for a while now, we just haven't been saying it all aloud. I get it. I really do."

She swallowed hard and added, "Things aren't going to work—between you and me."

Even as she said the words, a sense of loss nearly overwhelmed her.

Blaine nodded.

"I'm sorry," Riley said.

"You've got nothing to be sorry about," Blaine said.

Riley had to stop herself from saying, *"Oh, I do. I really do."*

After all, it was because of her own life choices that Blaine felt the way he did. Blaine had done his best to accept those choices. But in the end, he honestly couldn't do it. And Riley knew she had no one to blame but herself.

She and Blaine both fell silent for a little while. She was sitting on the couch, he in a chair facing her. She remembered the first time they had held hands, sitting on the couch right here. It had been a magical moment when she'd felt as if her life had suddenly changed for the better.

She wished they could hold hands right now. But she knew the distance between them was a lot greater than a few feet between two pieces of furniture.

Anyway, a decision seemed to have been made. She wasn't sure exactly what that decision was, and she doubted that Blaine did either. But something had ended between them. And there would be no getting it back again.

They began to talk a little, awkwardly and tentatively, about one thing and another. Blaine assured Riley that her family would always be welcome for free meals at his restaurant, and he'd be glad to see all of them.

And of course, they'd stay in close touch because of their daughters. April and Crystal were best friends, after all, and they'd be visiting each other a lot. And this wasn't like a divorce. They'd always stay close.

Blaine smiled weakly and added, "Maybe things won't be so different after all."

Riley blinked back a tear and said, "Maybe not."

But that wasn't true, and she knew it.

Then Blaine said he'd better get back to work, so they both got up and shyly kissed each other on the cheek, and Blaine left the house.

Riley muttered aloud to herself, "It's time for a drink."

She went to the kitchen and poured herself a glass of bourbon, then went back to the living room and sat down again. The house seemed ghostly quiet, and Riley felt deeply alone. And of course, she really *was* alone, even with three other people in nearby rooms. She cried softly for a few moments.

Then, after she dried her eyes and began to sip her bourbon, she tried to keep memories of happier times out of her mind. But she somehow couldn't manage it. She remembered the night when she and Blaine had first kissed on a dance floor while a band played her favorite song at his request. She remembered the first night they had slept together.

And she also remembered the two weeks that she, Blaine, and their three girls had spent together in a borrowed house on the shore at Sandbridge Beach. They really had felt like a whole family then. She especially remembered hearing the comforting soft rumble of waves on the night when Blaine had showed her architectural plans to enlarge his own home so they could all live together.

They really and truly had thought about getting married.

That had been little more than a month ago.

But it seems so long ago now.

Another, more discordant, memory crowded its way into her mind. It was Blaine telling her the morning after they'd first slept together, *"I think I need to buy a gun."*

And of course, he'd felt that need because of Riley and the dangers of being in a relationship with her. They'd gone to the gun store and bought him a Smith and Wesson 686, and Riley had given him his first shooting lesson at the indoor range right there and then.

Riley smiled bitterly as she thought, *I hope he takes better care of that gun than April did with hers.*

But then—what need would he have for that gun now that things were over between them?

What was he going to do with it?

Just leave it hidden away in his house and forget he even had it?

Or would he sell it?

As she considered these questions, an unexpected emotion crept up inside her. Her breath and pulse quickened, and to her surprise she realized, *I'm angry.*

She'd been blaming and doubting herself ever since Blaine's visit—even before then, really, when she'd found herself feeling at least somewhat guilty for April's accident with the gun.

But was everything that was going wrong in her life really her fault?

Riley growled under her breath as she took another sip of bourbon.

So many disappointments, she thought.

And she was tired of blaming herself for all of them—including the failure of her marriage to Ryan. Was it really her fault that Ryan had been an unfaithful, selfish jerk, and such a lousy husband and father? And was it her fault that April couldn't handle the responsibility of a gun, or that Jilly was angry with her for not getting one herself?

And was it really her fault that Blaine couldn't accept her for who she really was, that he wouldn't stay in a relationship with her unless she became somebody she couldn't possibly be? When she'd harbored such hopes of making a new life with him and his daughter, had she really been expecting too much from him? Wasn't true commitment always about accepting the good with the bad?

Wasn't it possible that Blaine was failing her, and not the other way around?

Now that Riley thought about it, she did have something to blame herself for. It was a single mistake she'd made over and over again in her life.

I trust people.

And sooner or later, people always failed to live up to that trust, no matter how hard she tried to live up to their demands and expectations.

Then Riley became aware of noises from the kitchen. Gabriela had come upstairs and was starting to fix dinner. Riley had to admit to herself, Gabriela was one person who had never let her down, never betrayed her trust.

And yet there were limits to her relationship with Gabriela. Although Gabriela was like another family member, since Riley was Gabriela's employer, they could only become just so close even as friends.

Gabriela started humming a Guatemalan melody in the kitchen, and Riley felt her anger start to ebb. Soon, she realized, she and Gabriela and the kids would sit down to a lovely dinner together.

Even if they were barely speaking to each other, that was a good thing.

She took another sip of bourbon and murmured aloud, "Life goes on."

Riley was awakened early the next morning by the sound of her phone buzzing on the nightstand. She picked up the phone groggily, but snapped awake when she saw that the call was from her boss, Brent Meredith.

"Did I wake you, Agent Paige?" Meredith asked in his gruff, rumbling voice.

Riley almost said no, but quickly thought better of it. It was always best to be truthful with Meredith, even about seemingly insignificant things. He had an uncanny way of detecting even the slightest dishonesty. And he really didn't like being lied to. Riley had found that out the hard way.

"Yes, but it's all right, sir," Riley said. "What can I do for you?"

"I was wondering if you might feel ready to get back on the job," Meredith said.

Riley sat up in bed, feeling more alert by the second.

What should I say? she wondered.

Even after supper yesterday, things were still strained between Riley and her two daughters. The girls were still sullen and distant. Was this really a good time to go back to work? Shouldn't she spend some time trying to work things out here at home?

"Is there a new case?" she asked.

"It looks like it," Meredith said. "There have been two murders in suburbs of Philadelphia during the last couple of weeks. Due to oddities in both crime scenes, the local cops think they must be related, and they've asked for our help. I know you've been resting up from your injury, and I don't want to—"

"I'll do it," Riley said, interrupting him.

The words were out before she even knew she'd said them.

"I'm glad to hear that," Meredith said. Then he added, "Agent Jeffreys is still on leave. I'll put Agent Roston on the job with you."

Riley almost objected. Right now she really wanted her long-time partner and best friend, Bill Jeffreys, with her, but then she remembered their recent phone conversations. He'd sounded pretty frayed, and with good reason. Bill had shot the man who had attacked Riley with an ice pick—shot him and killed him.

It wasn't the first person Bill or Riley had killed in the line of duty over the years, but Bill was taking it unusually hard. It was the first time he had used deadly force since he'd mistakenly shot an innocent man last April. That man had survived, but Bill was still haunted by his error.

"Agent Roston would be fine," Riley told Meredith. The young African American agent had become Riley's protégé during the last few months. Riley had come to think highly of her.

"I'll have a plane ready to fly out of Quantico to Philly as soon as you both can get here," Meredith said. "Meet me on the tarmac."

They ended the call, and Riley sat on the bed staring at the phone for a few moments.

Did I make the right decision? she wondered.

Should she really head on out like this when there was so much uncertainty here at home?

The question stirred up some of the same anger she'd felt yesterday.

Again, she resented having to think so much of other people's wants and needs—especially when they so often neglected to think about her.

She could stay here trying her best to placate April and Jilly, apologizing for things that weren't really her fault, or she could get out and do something useful. And right now, she had a job to do—a job that few if any other people could do as well as she could.

She looked at her clock and saw that it was still very early in the morning. She knew that Gabriela was already up getting breakfast ready, but the kids would still be in bed. Riley didn't feel much like explaining her decision to the kids, but she knew that Gabriela would understand if she went downstairs and told her. Riley could grab something to eat and head out, and Gabriela would tell the girls before sending them off to school.

Meanwhile, Riley had to get dressed and pack up her go-bag. As she got up from her bed and headed for the bathroom, she realized that she felt better than she had in days.

She'd soon be doing something she was good at—even if it could be extremely dangerous.

CHAPTER THREE

As the BAU plane took off from Quantico, Riley began to study the case files on her computer pad. She was about to comment on a particular point when she realized that Jenn Roston, sitting beside her, wasn't paying attention. Jenn was just staring out the window, apparently lost in her own thoughts.

"I guess we'd better get started," Riley said.

But she got no response from her young partner.

Riley said, "Did you hear me, Jenn?"

Again, there was no reply.

Then Riley spoke more sharply, "Jenn."

Jenn turned toward Riley with a startled expression.

"What?" she said.

It seemed to Riley almost as though Jenn had forgotten where she was.

What's going on with her? Riley wondered.

They had been in a rush to get on the plane just now. Meredith hadn't even called the two agents into his office for a briefing about the case. Instead, he'd met them on the airstrip tarmac beside the waiting plane. Just before they had boarded, Meredith hastily gave Riley instructions on how to download the relevant police reports. She'd barely gotten that done before takeoff.

Now, as the plane gained altitude, she expected to go over everything with her partner. But Jenn didn't seem to be her usual self.

With her dark skin, short straight hair, and large intense eyes, Riley's young partner looked like a woman who knew what she was doing. And she usually did, but today Jenn seemed distracted.

Riley pointed to her computer pad and said, "We've got a case to get started on."

Jenn nodded hastily and said, "I know. What have we got?"

As she skimmed the police reports, Riley said, "Not much, at least not yet. A week ago there was a murder in Petersboro, a Philadelphia suburb. Justin Selves, a husband and a father, was killed in his home. His throat was cut."

"What was the motive?" Jenn asked.

Riley said, "At first, the police there assumed that it was a burglary gone bad. Then just yesterday, a woman named Joan Cornell was found dead in her own home in Springett, a suburb right next to Petersboro. Her throat was cut as well."

Jenn tilted her head and said, "Maybe it was just another bungled robbery. The cause of death could just be coincidence. Sounds like it should be easy for the local cops to handle without our help. It doesn't sound like a serial."

Skimming the report further, Riley said, "Maybe not—except for one odd thing. A chair was stolen from each crime scene."

"A chair?" Jenn asked.

"Yes, a dining room chair."

"What kind of sense does that make?" Jenn demanded.

Riley said, "None yet, maybe. It's our job to make some sense of it."

Jenn shook her head and muttered, "Chairs. We're investigating stolen chairs."

Then she shrugged and added, "I'll bet it's nothing. Nothing for the BAU to look into, anyway. Just a couple of stupid and nasty murders. We'll probably be flying back to Quantico before we even know it."

Riley didn't know what to say. It wasn't her habit to form an opinion before a case was even underway. It wasn't like Jenn to do that either, but for some reason Jenn seemed uncharacteristically disengaged right now.

Riley said in a cautious voice, "Jenn, is anything wrong?"

"No," Jenn said. "Why do you ask?"

Riley fumbled for the right words to say.

"Well, it's just that … you seem kind of …"

Riley paused, then said, "You'd tell me if anything was wrong, wouldn't you?"

Jenn smiled weakly.

"What would be wrong?" she asked Riley. Then she turned and stared out the window again.

Riley felt an uneasy tingle at Jenn's evasive answer. She wondered—should she press the issue? Jenn could get touchy when people asked too many prying questions. Riley tried to convince herself that nothing was wrong at all. It might be just a fleeting mood on Jenn's part.

But still.

Riley knew a lot about Jenn—especially about her past. She knew that Jenn had grown up in a so-called "foster home" run by a brilliant and sinister woman who called herself "Aunt Cora." Aunt Cora had trained all her foster children for roles in her own crime network.

So far, Jenn had been the only foster kid to escape Aunt Cora's clutches. With her sharp mind and resolute personality, she had gained respect as a cop and then a BAU agent. But Riley knew that Aunt Cora had been in touch with Jenn during the time they had been working together. Those contacts had always seemed to disturb the young agent, but it had never kept her from doing her job.

What was going on now? Was Aunt Cora trying to lure Jenn back into her sphere of influence?

Surely she'd tell me, Riley thought.

The two had been wary of each other when they'd first worked together, but some dangerous cases had brought them much closer. They'd learned to trust each other with some pretty dark secrets. Jenn even knew more than Bill did about Riley's past entanglement with a criminal genius named Shane Hatcher.

Riley and Jenn had agreed not to hide anything important from each other. So now Riley hesitated to demand an explanation.

No, she decided. *I've got to trust her.*

Riley frowned at her own thought.

Her breakup with Blaine was still very fresh in her mind. So was April's irresponsible behavior with the gun, and Jilly's pouting over not getting a gun herself.

Riley sighed quietly and thought, *Trust is in kind of short supply for me right now.*

The plane was only in the air for an hour before it landed in the Philadelphia International Airport. There the agents were met by a cop who drove them north to Springett, a well-to-do Philadelphia suburb. The car stopped in front of a pleasant-looking three-story house, where a couple of other official vehicles were already parked.

Riley and Jenn got out of the car and walked toward the house. Their driver got out too and followed along behind them.

A white-haired uniformed man made his way out of the house and past the police tape across the front porch. He introduced himself as Jeremy Kree, the chief of police in nearby Petersboro, where the first murder had happened.

While shaking his hand, Riley said, "Agent Roston and I will be needing a vehicle to get around in while we're in the area."

Kree nodded and said, "You can use the car that brought you here."

He told the cop who had driven them to lend them the keys to the unmarked vehicle. Then he ushered Riley and Jenn inside the house and introduced them to Burton Shore, a younger man who was the police chief here in Springett. Burton led them toward the area where the murder had taken place.

The first thing to catch Riley's attention was the dining room table, a new-looking square design with chairs placed on three of its sides. According to the report she'd read, a fourth chair was originally part of the set but had been stolen. The table itself struck her as small for such a large family home. It looked rather odd in the wide dining area.

Probably an insignificant detail, Riley thought.

Still, it bothered her, and she wasn't sure why.

Shore escorted them around a marble-topped counter with a telltale bloodstain on its edge. There on the kitchen floor was a taped outline where the victim's body had fallen. A large pool of brownish blood on the tile floor had mostly coagulated but still appeared to be somewhat damp.

Riley asked Chief Shore, "When was the body taken away?"

"The county coroner ordered it to be removed last night. He wanted to get started on an autopsy as soon as he could. I assume that was all right."

Riley nodded. She would have preferred for the crime scene to be as undisturbed as possible when she and Jenn had arrived. But the coroner's decision hadn't been unreasonable, especially since they hadn't made an immediate connection with the earlier murder.

She asked both chiefs, "What have you got in the way of photos?"

Chief Shore opened a folder to show pictures of the crime scene right here where Joan Cornell's body had been found, and Chief Kree got out photos of the other slain victim. Riley and Jenn pored over the images silently for a moment.

Both victims had wounds on their foreheads, suggesting that they had had been hit and at least stunned before the fatal wounds to their throats had been delivered. Judging from the stain right here on the counter, Riley guessed that the killer must have banged the woman's head on its edge, then cut her throat as she lay on the kitchen floor.

Riley felt an eerie chill of déjà vu at the sight of the gaping throat wounds and copious blood. They reminded her of the first case she'd ever worked on, before she'd even considered becoming an FBI agent. It had been years ago, back when she was a student at Lanton University. A murderer had killed two of her friends by cutting their throats in their dorm rooms. Riley had gotten sucked into the investigation reluctantly, and her life had never been the same.

Riley quickly shook off that feeling.

New killer, different time, she told herself.

She asked Chief Shore, "What do we know about the murder that happened right here?"

The young chief said, "The victim's name was Joan Cornell, and she was a divorced mother of four. Three of her children live around the country, but her oldest child, a daughter, still lives here in Springett. The daughter has always stopped in fairly regularly to check in on her mother. Yesterday afternoon she found her dead, right here."

Jenn asked, "Does the victim's ex-husband live near here?"

Chief Shore shook his head and said, "No, he's remarried and living up in Maine. We've been in touch with him, and he's accounted for his whereabouts at the time of the murder. We'll check his alibi, but I'm pretty sure it will hold up."

Riley silently agreed. Somehow, this murder didn't seem like the act of an angry ex-husband, especially one who lived so far away. And certainly not if these deaths in two different families were as closely connected as they appeared to be.

Jenn looked up from the pictures to the older police chief.

She asked him, "What do we know about the first victim?"

Chief Kree said, "His name was Justin Selves, and he worked as a customer service rep at a local bank over in Petersboro. His son came home one afternoon a couple of weeks ago and found his father dead just inside the front door to his house."

Jenn asked, "Was there any sign of a break-in?"

Kree said, "No, it appears that Selves simply answered the door when the killer knocked or rang. Then the killer made his way inside and committed the murder right there and then."

Riley pointed to one of the pictures where a bloodstained spot was visible on a doorframe and said, "It looks like he was knocked unconscious, just like the victim was here."

Kree nodded. "Yeah, his head seems to have been smashed against the doorframe, probably when the door was closed."

As Jenn continued questioning the two chiefs, Riley stood for a moment staring at the taped outline on the floor. Her greatest strength as an agent was her almost uncanny ability to get inside a killer's mind while studying a crime scene. But that didn't happen every time, and it wasn't happening right now. So far, her mind felt blank.

Jenn seemed well engaged now and was asking the two police chiefs all the necessary routine questions. Riley knew that Jenn wasn't likely to get any breakthrough answers. This seemed to Riley like as good a time as any to go exploring through the house and maybe get some kind of an intuitive hit as to what had happened here.

As Riley roamed around the ground floor, she peeked down into the finished basement, which appeared to be mostly a large recreation room. She wandered on through a breakfast room and a large living room with a nice fireplace. There were a number of family pictures arranged on the piano and elsewhere—all of them showing the mother and her four kids at different ages, but none of her ex-husband.

Hardly surprising, Riley thought.

She certainly didn't keep any photos of Ryan in view in her own house.

Riley continued on upstairs to the second and third floors, where she saw that the children's bedrooms seemed to have been kept pretty much as they must have been when the kids had still lived here.

She remembered Chief Shore mentioning the one daughter who lived nearby and visited the victim regularly, and who had found the body. Riley wondered how much the murdered woman had seen of her other children since they'd grown up and moved away. In a broken family like this, she doubted that everybody regularly got together even for the holidays.

It was a sad thought. Although the house was a good bit larger than Riley's home, it still made her wonder, *What will it be like when April and Jilly are gone?*

Would they both live far away and seldom visit?

And of course, Gabriela also wouldn't be around forever.

What would Riley's life be like then?

Would she feel alone and forgotten?

If something awful were to happen to her at home, how long might it be before anyone even came around to find out about it?

Riley was back downstairs now, looking into the dining room. Once again, the small square table with its three chairs seemed much too small for the space. And again, Riley found it an oddly unsettling sight. She felt sure that it had been bought to replace another much larger table that harbored too many memories for Joan Cornell to live with.

Riley felt a lump form in her throat as she thought about Joan Cornell's lonely existence—and how horribly it had ended.

Her thoughts were interrupted by the sound of Jenn saying sharply, "You don't know what you're talking about."

Riley turned and saw that Jenn was talking heatedly with Chief Shore while his older colleague stood staring at the two of them with a bemused expression.

"There was no struggle here," Jenn continued, pacing the kitchen area. "There's no sign of any struggle at all, no damage to anything in the kitchen. The killer took her completely by surprise. He grabbed her suddenly—by the hair, maybe—and slammed her head against the countertop right here. Then he cut her throat. She never knew what had happened."

"But how—?" Chief Shore began.

Jenn interrupted, "How did he do it? Maybe like this."

Jenn walked around and stood at the side of the counter nearer to Riley, the side that faced the dining room.

Jenn said, "He might have been standing right where I'm standing. Maybe he asked the victim for a glass of water. She walked into the kitchen area, and he reached across the counter, and..."

She pantomimed the killer grabbing the woman by the hair and pulling her head forward and bashing it against the counter.

"That's how it happened, I'll bet," Jenn said. "You should ask the coroner to check out the victim's scalp, see if any hair was pulled."

Chief Shore squinted at Jenn and said, "So what are you saying? That the victim knew her killer? That she trusted him?"

Jenn snapped at him, "I don't know. Maybe that's something you should try to figure out. Maybe it's something you should *investigate*."

Riley was alarmed by the biting sarcasm in Jenn's voice. She'd seen this kind of behavior from Jenn before, and of course it was never a good way to start working with local cops. Riley knew she had to put a stop to it right now.

Before her younger partner could say anything else, Riley spoke up sharply, "Agent Roston."

Jenn turned toward her with a surprised expression on her face.

Trying to act as though she wasn't deliberately interrupting, Riley said to her, "I think we've seen all we need to see here. Let's move on."

Then Riley said to Chief Shore, "I'd like to interview the victim's daughter—the one who found the body. Do you have any idea how I might reach her?"

Shore nodded and said, "She told me yesterday she'd be staying home from work today. I can give you her address and directions for getting there."

Riley listened and jotted down the address and directions. She exchanged phone numbers with the cops so they could all stay in close touch. Then Riley thanked them for their help, and she and Jenn left the house.

As they walked toward their borrowed vehicle, Riley snapped at Jenn, "What did you think you were doing back there?"

Jenn growled, "Straightening them out, that's all. Those two guys don't know what they're doing. They ought to be able to solve this all by themselves before the day is over. They shouldn't need our help. We're wasting our time and taxpayers' money."

"We're BAU," Riley said. "Helping local authorities is a big part of what we do."

"Yeah, on serious cases, like real serial killers," Jenn said. "This isn't that kind of a case, and I think we both know it. It's just some stupid burglar who's liable to trip himself up and get caught before he does anybody else any harm."

As they climbed into the car and Riley turned on the ignition, she stopped herself from saying, *"I don't know anything of the kind."*

In fact, she had a pretty strong feeling that the two murders were just the start of something really ugly.

CHAPTER FOUR

As Riley began to drive through Springett, she decided she needed to be blunt. She told Jenn, "You may have caused us a setback."

Jenn growled something inaudible under her breath.

"We're here to help the local cops, not argue with them," Riley told her. "Maintaining mutual trust can be tricky under the best of circumstances. And it's damned important. You were way out of line back there."

"Come on, Riley," Jenn snapped. "Shore was flat out wrong about what happened. Did *you* see any sign of a struggle in that kitchen?"

"That's not the point," Riley said. "We still need to work with him. And besides, based on your own observations, I think your conclusions are faulty."

"Yeah? How so?"

Riley shrugged. "You said yourself that the killer moved swiftly and took Joan Cornell completely unawares. It probably happened just like you said it did. He reached across the counter and grabbed her by the hair and slammed her head onto the counter."

Following Chief Shore's directions, Riley turned at a stoplight. "Then he walked behind the counter," she continued, "and cut her throat while she was unconscious. And judging from the photos of the crime scene in Petersboro, he killed Justin Selves pretty much exactly the same way, with surprise and efficiency. Does that really sound like a botched burglary to you?"

"No," Jenn grumbled.

"Not to me either," Riley said. "In fact, it sounds pretty cold-blooded, even premeditated."

Silence fell between them as Riley drove through the well-to-do neighborhood. Riley's worries were mounting.

Finally she said, "Jenn, I asked you before, and I need to ask you again. Is something wrong that I should know about?"

"What would be wrong?" Jenn said.

Riley grimaced to hear the same evasive answer as before.

I'd better get right to the point, she thought.

"Has Aunt Cora been in touch with you?" she asked.

There was a pause as Jenn turned and stared at Riley.

"What kind of a question is that?" Jenn asked.

Riley said, "An easy one to answer, that's what kind of question it is. Yes or no. Either you've heard from her or you haven't."

Sensing that Jenn was about to protest, Riley added, "And don't tell me it's none of my business. You and I know things about each other that we'd rather nobody else knew. We've both got to be open about everything. And you're my partner, and something seems to be bothering you, and I'm worried it might affect your work. That makes it my business."

Jenn stared out at the street for a moment.

"No," she finally said.

"You mean, no, she hasn't been in touch with you?" Riley said.

"That's right," Jenn said.

"And you'd tell me if she had been?"

Jenn let out a slight gasp.

"Of course I'd tell you," she said. "You know I would. How could you think otherwise?"

"OK," Riley said.

They fell silent again as Riley kept on driving. She thought that Jenn had sounded perfectly sincere, and even a little hurt that she could doubt her. Riley wanted to trust her. But despite all that Jenn had achieved in her young life, it was hard to ignore the fact that she had once been apprenticed to be a master criminal.

But maybe I'm overreacting.

Again, she reminded herself of all that had happened yesterday at home. After April's carelessness with the gun, Riley simply wasn't in a very trusting mood. Maybe she was letting her own low spirits get the best of her. She told herself, *Don't start getting paranoid.*

Still, she thought maybe she should have insisted on bringing in Bill when Meredith had called her about the case. She was sure that Bill had been through much worse crises than whatever he was going through right now. Surely he could have snapped out of this one if Riley had pressed the issue. He was her oldest and best friend. Having him around always made Riley feel more anchored and secure.

As things stood, she simply had to make the best of things.

Soon they arrived at the address they'd been given. Riley parked the car in front of an old and elegant red brick apartment building. They got out of the car, walked up to the front entrance, and buzzed the apartment number. When a woman's voice answered over the speaker, Riley said, "Ms. Tovar, I'm Agent Riley Paige with the FBI, and I'm here with my partner, Jenn Roston. We'd like to come in and talk to you, if you don't mind."

The voice sputtered, "FBI? I—I hadn't expected..."

After a pause, the woman buzzed Riley and Jenn in. Riley and Jenn climbed the stairs to the second floor and knocked on the apartment door. The door opened to reveal a woman in her twenties standing there in her slippers and bathrobe. Riley couldn't tell from Lori Tovar's haggard expression whether she had been asleep or crying. The woman barely glanced at their IDs, then invited Riley and Jenn to come in and sit down.

As they made their way toward a cluster of sofas and chairs, Riley glanced around at the spacious apartment. In contrast to the building's venerable exterior, the apartment looked sleek and modern and had obviously been upgraded in recent years.

It also struck Riley as strangely empty and austere. The furniture looked expensive and tastefully simple, but there wasn't much of it, nor were there many paintings or decorations to be seen. Everything seemed so...

Tentative, Riley thought.

It felt almost as though the people who lived here had never really settled in.

As Lori Tovar sat facing Riley and Jenn, she said, "The police asked me so many questions. I told them all I could. I can't imagine ... what else you could want to know."

"Let's start from the beginning," Riley said. "How did you find out what had happened to your mother?"

Lori inhaled sharply.

She said, "It was yesterday, late in the afternoon. I just stopped by to check in on her."

"Did you visit her often?" Jenn asked.

Lori sighed and said, "As often as I could. I'm—I was pretty much all she had left. Dad left her a few years ago, and my brothers and sister all live too far away. Yesterday I got off work early—I'm a nurse at South Hill Hospital here in Springett—so I decided to stop by and see how she was doing. She'd been feeling pretty low lately."

Lori stared off into space for a moment, then continued, "When I got there, I found the front door was unlocked, which worried me. Then I came on inside."

Her voice faded away. Riley leaned toward her a little and said in a gentle voice, "Did you find her right away? The first thing when you came into the house, I mean?"

"No," Lori said. "I called out for her when I came inside, and she didn't answer. I went upstairs to see if she was taking a nap, but she wasn't in her bedroom. I thought—I hoped—she'd gone out on her own with friends. I went back downstairs, and ..."

Lori's forehead knotted with thought.

"I looked into the dining room and noticed that one of the chairs at the table was missing. That seemed odd. Then I saw a stain on the kitchen counter, and I went and looked into the kitchen, and ..."

She shuddered violently, and her voice became strained.

"And there she was lying on the floor. What happened after that is kind of a blur. I vaguely remember calling nine-one-one, then waiting for what seemed like a long time, but it was probably only a few minutes, and the police arrived, and ..."

Her voice faded away again.

Then, speaking more calmly, she said, "I don't know why I went into shock like that. I've seen terrible things in my job, especially in the emergency room. Awful wounds, lots of blood, people dying in horrible pain, or wishing they could die until we could manage their pain. I've always been able to deal with it. Even when I saw my first dead body, I didn't react like that. I should have handled it better."

Jenn glanced over at Riley with a curious expression. Riley guessed that Jenn was puzzled by the seeming detachment in Lori's voice. But Riley was pretty sure she understood.

Over the years, Riley had dealt with many people who were suffering from freshly traumatic experiences. She knew that this woman was still trying to process the reality of what had happened. Lori hadn't yet fully come to grips with the fact that it was her *mother* who had been murdered, not some emergency room patient she'd never met before.

Most of all, Lori hadn't accepted that there were limits to her own stoicism.

Riley wondered—were there people in Lori's life who would help her come to terms with all that?

She said to Lori, "I understand that you're married."

Lori nodded numbly.

"Roy owns a CPA firm here in Springett. He offered to stay home with me today, but I told him I'd be fine, and he should go on in to work."

Then with a slight shrug she added, "Life goes on."

Riley was startled to hear Lori say the very same words she'd spoken aloud to herself yesterday after Blaine had left the house. Hearing someone else say them was jarring. It made Riley realize how truly cliché the phrase really was. Worse still, *It's not even true.*

Riley's whole life had been built on the awful fact that all life ended in death sooner or later.

So why did people keep saying it?

Why had *she* said it herself just yesterday?

Just one of those lies we cling to, I guess.

Lori glanced back and forth between Jenn and Riley and said, "The police told me there was another victim a couple of weeks ago—a man over in Petersboro."

"That's right," Jenn said.

Lori added, "They said a chair was missing from *his* dining room set, just like with Mom. I don't understand. What does that mean? Why would anyone kill somebody over a dining room chair?"

Riley didn't reply, and neither did Jenn.

After all, how could they answer such a question?

Was it possible that they were really looking for some maniac who killed people for their furniture? It seemed too absurd to believe. But there was so little that they knew at this point in their investigation.

Jenn asked the next question.

"Did your mother happen to know a certain Justin Selves over in Petersboro?"

"Was that the other victim?" Lori asked.

Jenn nodded.

Lori squinted and said, "The name doesn't ring a bell. I don't know that she had any friends or acquaintances outside of Springett. I kept telling her she didn't get out enough. She didn't spend enough time with people."

Riley said, "I take it she didn't work outside the house."

Lori said, "No, she's been living off her divorce settlement."

Jenn asked, "Was your mother...dating anybody?"

Lori chuckled sadly.

"Lord, no. I think she'd have told me if she were. She seldom left the house except to go to church services once in a while. Oh, and she also went to the church's bingo games. She never missed those. There's a game every Friday evening at Westminster Presbyterian. She treated me to some cupcakes that she won there one night. She was very happy about that."

Lori shook her head again and said, "She spent too much time by herself. That house was too big for her. I kept telling her she should move someplace smaller. She wouldn't listen."

"What's going to happen to the house?" Jenn asked.

Lori sighed and said, "My sister and brothers and I will inherit it. That won't mean much to them. Since they live so far away, I guess it'll be pretty much mine now."

Then her eyes narrowed as if some especially dark thought had just crossed her mind.

"The house will be mine," she repeated. "And Roy's."

She hastily got up from her chair.

"If you don't mind, I'd rather not answer any more questions."

Riley sensed a sudden change in Lori's mood. She glanced around the large but oddly austere apartment again, then remembered the spacious house where the victim had been murdered. And something started to dawn on her.

Jenn craned forward and said, "Ma'am, if you could give us just a couple more minutes—"

"No," Lori interrupted. "No, I'd like to be alone now."

Riley could tell that Jenn had also picked up on the change in Lori's demeanor. Riley also knew that her partner would press the woman for answers—perhaps too aggressively.

Riley stood up and said, "Thank you for your time, Ms. Tovar. We're deeply sorry for your loss."

The woman sighed and said, "Thank you." Then she added yet again, "Life goes on."

If only that were true, Riley thought. *Or at least, not so briefly.*

As she and her partner headed out of the apartment and down the stairs, Jenn complained, "Why did we leave? There was something she wasn't telling us."

I know, Riley thought.

But she had no intention of making Lori Tovar tell them what it was.

"I'll explain it to you in the car," Riley said.

Chapter Five

As Riley drove away from Lori Tovar's apartment building, she realized her young partner was still agitated. In fact, Jenn had been rather short-tempered all day and Riley was feeling impatient with her attitude.

"What's the hurry?" Jenn grumbled. "Why did you get us out of there so fast?"

When Riley didn't answer right away, Jenn demanded, "Where are we going, anyway?"

"To find someplace to eat," Riley said with a shrug. "I haven't had anything to eat since breakfast, so I'm hungry. Aren't you?"

"I think we should go back there," Jenn said. "Lori Tovar wasn't telling us everything she knew."

Riley smiled grimly.

"What do you think she wasn't telling us?" she said.

"I don't know," Jenn said. "That's what I want to find out. Don't you? Sometimes witnesses can be reluctant about important things. Maybe she knew about some connection between her mother and a possible suspect—something she didn't want to tell us for some reason."

Riley replied, "Oh, there was something she didn't want to tell us, all right. But it wasn't anything we needed to know. It didn't have anything to do with the case."

"How do you know?" Jenn asked.

Riley stifled a sigh. She told herself not to be annoyed at Jenn for not picking up the same signals she had. Riley herself would probably have missed them when she was Jenn's age. Still, Jenn needed to learn how to read people better. She was often too quick to assign blame.

She said, "Tell me, Jenn—what were your impressions of Lori Tovar's apartment?"

Jenn shrugged. "It looked pretty expensive. The kind of place where a successful CPA and his wife might live. But very simple. Contemporary, I guess you'd call it."

"Would you say that Lori and her husband were very settled there?"

Jenn thought for a moment, then said, "Now that you mention it, I guess not. It sort of seemed like—I don't know, like maybe they hadn't added much beyond the basics. I guess I mean they hadn't really personalized it. Like they didn't expect to live there a lot longer."

Riley said, "And why might that be?"

When Jenn didn't answer, Riley prompted her, "What kind of plans do you think a couple like that would have for the near future?"

"Children," Jenn said.

Then came a pause, and Jenn added, "Oh. I think I'm getting it. They never meant to have kids while they were still living in that apartment. They wanted to move into someplace more family-like. Lori was hoping to wind up with her mother's house. And now..."

Riley nodded and said, "And now she's getting exactly what she wished for."

Jenn gasped a little.

"My God! I can't imagine how guilty she must feel!"

"Too guilty to ever live in that house, I imagine," Riley said. "She and her siblings are probably going to wind up having to sell the place, with all its wonderful childhood memories. And Lori and her husband will have to put off starting a family until they find another dream house. It's going to be hard for her."

"No wonder she didn't want to talk about it," Jenn said.

"Right," Riley said. "And it really was none of our business."

"I'm sorry," Jenn said. "I was being really stupid."

"You just have to learn how to pay better attention to *people*," Riley said. "And that means more than just getting information out of them. In means being able to empathize with them. It means respecting their feelings."

"I'll try to remember that," Jenn said quietly.

Riley felt encouraged that Jenn wasn't being defensive now. In fact, her partner seemed to have snapped out of her peculiar mood. Maybe, Riley thought, they'd wind up working just fine together after all.

Riley drove into downtown Springett and parked on its main street. She and Jenn got out and walked around until they found a pleasant little restaurant. They went inside and sat down in a fairly isolated booth and ordered sandwiches.

While they waited for their food, Jenn asked, "So where does this leave us now?"

"I wish I knew," Riley said.

"We're too short of witnesses," Jenn said. "It would help if someone—a nosy neighbor, maybe—had seen the killer when he showed up at those houses, or at least his vehicle. We need a description of some kind. But while you were looking around the house, I asked the two police chiefs if they'd interviewed the victims' neighbors. They had, and nobody had seen anything. There weren't any security cameras in the right places either."

Riley already knew this from reading the police reports.

Jenn continued, "We *do* know there wasn't any kind of a break-in at either of the two houses. What does that tell us?"

"I'm not sure," Riley said. "From what Lori Tovar said, maybe her mother had just forgotten to lock the door. The killer might have taken her by surprise once he was inside."

Jenn said, "The other crime scene was different. Justin Selves was knocked out and killed right next to his own front door. Maybe the killer walked up to the house and knocked or rang the door-bell, and Selves answered and let him come right on in."

"The same thing might have happened with Joan Cornell," Riley agreed.

Jenn said, "Yeah, and maybe she even spent a little while talking with the killer before he got around to killing her. So I guess you're right that the victims already knew and trusted their killer."

"Maybe," Riley said. "But it's still possible that he was a total stranger, just probably not a random burglar. Don't forget, lots of psychopaths are perfectly charming people. Maybe the two victims trusted him the minute they first met him at the door. Maybe he seemed like a perfectly nice guy who claimed to be taking a survey or something. So they let him come inside."

Jenn said, "Well, this killer's got a lot of daring, that much seems sure. Walking right into those houses in broad daylight like that took some nerve. Do you think maybe we should go take a look at the first crime scene?"

"I don't think we'll learn anything there," Riley said. "It was two whole weeks ago, and at the time the police just thought it was some sort of burglary gone wrong. Everything's been cleaned up there by now."

"You're right, there won't be anything to see," Jenn said. "Nothing that the photos don't show."

Riley said, "But we do know that Selves's son discovered his body. We should definitely talk to him."

Riley looked up the police reports on her computer pad and found the son's phone number. Then she called him on her cell phone and put the call on speaker so Jenn could join in.

The young man's name was Ian, and he seemed more than eager to talk to a couple of FBI agents.

"What happened to Dad has been driving me crazy," he said. "Especially since the police called this morning and told me it had happened to somebody else over in Springett. A woman got killed this time. I can't believe this. What the hell is going on?"

"We're hoping you can help us find out," Riley said. "We'd like to ask you some questions. Is there someplace we could meet? We're in downtown Springett right now."

"Well, I'm a student at Temple University, and I'm on campus between classes at the moment. I don't figure you want to spend a lot of time driving through Philly just to talk to me. Could we just Skype?"

That sounded like a good idea to Riley. A few moments later, Jenn and Riley sat side by side in the booth talking face to face with Ian Selves. The server brought them their sandwiches, but they pushed them aside for the time being.

Riley noticed right away that Ian had a pleasantly bookish face that reminded her of some of the lab technicians she often worked with at the BAU. He looked about eighteen or nineteen, and Riley guessed that he was maybe a sophomore studying physics or engineering or computer science.

Jenn asked him the same question Riley had asked Lori Tovar at the start of their interview. "How did you find out what had happened to your father?"

Ian said, "Well, as you probably know, Dad was a customer service rep at a bank in Petersboro. Once every week we always met for lunch during his lunch break. He'd drive home from work, and I'd drive by and pick him up, and we'd go someplace where we liked to eat."

Riley was pleased by Ian's clarity. Unlike Lori Tovar, he'd had two weeks to process what had happened, and he could talk about it calmly.

A better witness, she thought.

Ian continued, "I stopped my car in front of the house and honked my horn, but Dad didn't come out. That wasn't like him at all. So I got out of the car and went up to the house and knocked on the door, and he didn't answer."

Ian shook his head.

"I started really worrying right then. If Dad had made other plans, he'd have certainly let me know. I figured something had to be wrong. So I opened the door and ..."

Ian visibly shuddered at the memory.

"There he was, lying on the floor."

Jenn asked, "What did you do then?"

"Well, I freaked out for a minute or two, I guess. But I called nine-one-one as soon as I could pull myself together. Then I called my mom. She works at a women's clothing store—Rochelle's Boutique. I told her something bad had happened to Dad. She figured out right away that I meant that Dad was dead. I didn't tell her how or why. At that point, I really didn't really know myself."

Ian sighed and went on. "She pretty much lost it on the phone. I knew that it would be really bad if she came right home. I told her to go over to her sister's house after work and wait there until I could really explain everything. So she wasn't at home while the police came and asked all kinds of questions and the county coroner took the body away. I think it was probably just as well."

Yes, I'm sure it was, Riley thought.

She found herself impressed by the young man's cool decision-making in the midst of such a traumatic ordeal.

Jenn asked him, "When did you notice that a dining room chair was missing?"

Ian said, "Well, as you know, the cops thought the whole thing was some kind of a bungled burglary. Like maybe the guy didn't expect anybody to be home, and he was surprised that Dad was there."

Stroking his chin, he added, "So the cops asked me right then and there if any valuables were missing. I went through the whole house checking everything I could think of—computers, TVs, Mom's jewelry, the silverware and china, all that kind of stuff. I finally noticed the missing chair."

He squinted with disbelief.

"The cops told me this morning that a chair got stolen from the other victim. That doesn't make sense. Why would anybody kill somebody over a chair?"

Riley remembered Lori Tovar asking exactly the same question. She still had no idea what the answer was.

Jenn asked Ian, "The other victim's name was Joan Cornell. Did your father ever mention somebody by that name?"

Ian shook his head.

"I don't think so, but I'm not sure. He was pretty outgoing. Mom is more shy, a real stay-at-home type. But Dad went out a lot and socialized, played bridge and softball and belonged to a bowling team and took an aerobics class, so he knew a lot of people. He might have mentioned her and I forgot."

An idea was starting to take shape in Riley's mind.

"Did he ever mention playing bingo?" she said.

Ian's eyes widened a little.

"Now that you mention it, yeah," he said. "It was at some church. He wasn't actually a church-going kind of guy so I guess it was somewhere he went just for the games."

"Did he say what this church was?" Jenn asked.

He was silent for a moment, then added, "Nope, can't remember his actually mentioning that. But one day he told me he didn't want to go there anymore."

"Did he say why?" Riley asked.

"No."

Riley exchanged glances with Jenn.

Jenn asked, "How long ago did he tell you that?"

Ian shrugged and said, "Just a few days before he was killed, I think."

"Thanks for your time," Riley said. "You've been very helpful."

"And we're very sorry for your loss," Jenn added.

"Thanks," Ian said. "I'm coping OK, I guess, but this is really hard on Mom. I'm her only kid, and it's hard for her to be living alone in that house now. I offered to drop out of school for a semester and stay with her, but she won't hear of it. I worry a lot about her."

Riley wished him well and thanked him again and ended the chat session.

"So both victims might have played bingo together at a church," Jenn said. "That's our next stop."

Riley agreed. She looked up the phone number for Westminster Presbyterian Church and made the call. She asked the receptionist who answered the phone who was in charge of the church's bingo games. The receptionist immediately connected Riley with the church's activity director, Buddy Sears. When Riley and Jenn introduced themselves as FBI agents, Sears said, "This sounds very serious. May I ask what this is all about?"

Riley asked him if he knew Joan Cornell.

"Why, yes. A lovely woman. One of our regulars. Why do you ask?"

Riley and Jenn exchanged looks again. Riley knew that she and her partner were thinking the same thing: *He doesn't know she's been murdered.*

This phone call wouldn't be a good way for him to find out. She decided not to bring up Selves's name right now.

Riley said to Sears, "We'd like to talk with you in person, if you don't mind. Are you available this afternoon?"

"Why, of course," the man said, sounding worried now. "I'll be right here waiting to see you."

Riley thanked him and ended the call. As Riley and Jenn hastily resumed eating their sandwiches, Jenn said, "This is it, Riley. This is the connection we're looking for. If both victims were at that church, the killer must have been there too."

I hope so, Riley thought.

But after years of experience, she knew that there was still a lot to be learned about this case.

CHAPTER SIX

Drew Cadigan knew exactly what she wanted right now. She opened the little freezer compartment of her refrigerator and located the treat she was looking for. The compartment was a little hard to close tight again, because the refrigerator needed to be defrosted—and cleaned as well.

Like that's going to happen anytime soon! she thought with a grin.

She knew that most of the off-campus apartments rented by her fellow students boasted newer appliances, including refrigerators that self-defrosted. But she and her roommate, Sylvia, had both been glad to find this less expensive place in a big, older house that had been remodeled for apartments.

Fortunately, she and Sylvia were on the same wavelength in a lot of ways. Neither one of them was exactly inclined to keep things clean, tidy, neat, and in proper working order. Neither one of them minded that the apartment they shared was pretty much a wreck all the time.

Drew grabbed a tablespoon out of a kitchen drawer and carried it and the carton of chocolate chip cookie dough ice cream over to the nice little kitchen table she and Sylvia had bought when they'd moved in here over the summer. She put the carton and the spoon on the table and sat down on one of the simple straight-back chairs they'd bought with the table.

A smart purchase, she thought.

She and Sylvia had picked up the chairs and the table at the This-and-That Thrift Store. Really, they looked as nice as the brand new and considerably more expensive sets at Wolfe's Furniture, where Drew had worked as a salesperson over the summer.

Thinking of the customers she'd served there, she murmured aloud, "What suckers."

Of course, those people were all a lot better off than Drew or her family had ever been, so they didn't know any better. Ever since Drew was a little girl, her mother had taught her that you could buy excellent things at a good thrift store. The table and chairs were a good example. So were just about all of Drew's clothes.

And clothes were important here at Springett College, where just about everybody was a whole lot richer than Drew. She had to at least put on the appearance of affluence, even if everybody around her knew better than to think she had any money.

She pulled open the carton and sat staring at the ice cream for a moment, her tablespoon poised to attack its untouched creamy surface.

Should I? she wondered.

No, of course she shouldn't. She and Sylvia had agreed to save it and share it for some special celebration.

But Drew was having a special moment right now, and Sylvia wasn't here.

Just one bite, she thought.

She dipped the tablespoon into the hard surface and scooped out a lump of the stuff containing a soft morsel of cookie dough. She closed her eyes and savored the heavenly cold sweetness.

I deserve this, she decided.

Drew was sure that Sylvia would forgive her when she told her what she was celebrating. She had just survived her first quiz in her Survey of American Literature course. In fact, she was sure she'd done really well on it.

And that really was cause for celebration.

By the end of her freshman year last spring, she'd begun to doubt that she could even survive at Springett. Not because she wasn't smart enough. Her excellent standardized test scores and high school academic record had gotten her a hefty scholarship, making it possible for her to come here.

Even so, she'd found it hard to compete during her first two semesters, and she was at risk of losing that scholarship. She was surrounded by rich kids who could afford all sorts of academic help. That put Drew at a distinct disadvantage—especially during a required seminar in critical thinking in the spring semester.

She'd chosen a seminar entitled, ironically enough, Poverty and Affluence in American Culture. Everybody at the seminar table talked circles around her, sometimes using academic jargon she'd never heard before. They were all getting daily tutoring for the seminar, and she couldn't keep up with them. And their term papers had been so polished that she doubted her classmates had even written them.

Remembering her ordeal, she thought, *I learned a lot about poverty and affluence, that's for sure.*

Drew had barely survived that first year, but she'd learned some important lessons along the way. So had Sylvia, who wasn't rich either and had suffered from the same sorts of problems.

As soon as they'd rented this place last June, they'd started studying way ahead for all their courses in the coming fall. Drew's summer furniture store job had allowed her plenty of time to read. She'd plowed through all the assigned texts for her Survey of American Lit class, including such formidable tomes as *The Scarlet Letter* and *Moby-Dick* and the complete *Leaves of Grass*.

Sylvia had taken the same approach to her own major in anthropology, reading all the textbooks she could get her hands on. More importantly, Drew and Sylvia had tutored each other, staying up late at night and drilling each other mercilessly all summer long. By the time this semester started, they'd joked that they could easily take each other's classes or even exchange majors if they felt like it.

And now, after the quiz she'd taken just a little while ago, Drew felt sure that all that hard work was going to pay off. Her rich, tutor-pampered rivals were going to have to struggle to keep up with *her* for a change.

Yes, she had every right to celebrate.

As she sat staring at the carton contemplating whether to take another bite of ice cream, she was startled by a voice.

"Excuse me."

She looked up and saw a man she didn't know standing in her apartment doorway.

I shouldn't have left the door open, she thought.

But everybody in the apartment house did that pretty much all the time. Delivery people and strangers stopped at the front door of the building and rang a bell for the apartment they wanted.

In an apologetic tone, the man said, "I didn't mean to startle you. I guess the front door to the house is supposed to stay locked. But somebody put duct tape over the latch, so just anybody can come right in. That might not be such a good idea."

No, it's not a good idea, Drew thought.

But some of her housemates kept taping the door that way, either to save themselves the trouble of using their keys or to let their friends come and go whenever they wanted. Drew and Sylvia had both complained to their neighbors about that, to no avail.

The man said, "I'm looking for Maureen. Doesn't she live here?"

Drew shook her head silently.

The man said, "Oh, I'm sorry, my mistake."

Glancing out the door into the hallway, he added, "I suppose she must live in one of the other apartments."

Drew felt herself relax a little. The man seemed harmless and even pleasant, just rather confused.

She said, "I'm afraid nobody named Maureen lives here."

"Are you sure?" the man said. "Everybody calls her Mo."

"No, nobody named Mo either. Sorry."

He tilted his head and said, "Maybe you just don't know her. Maybe she just moved in and you haven't met her yet."

"No. I know everybody in the house."

The man gazed at her with a strangely knowing look.

"I see," he said.

Drew felt a renewed chill. He sounded as though he didn't believe her.

Why would I lie about something like that? she wondered.

And why didn't he just leave, now that he knew the person he was looking for didn't live here?

Then he smiled at the carton on the table and said, "I see you still like your ice cream."

Drew was jolted by confusion.

Still?

What did he mean by *still?*

Then he glanced around the apartment.

"But, my goodness! You used to be so neat and orderly. I even used to tease you about it. And you teased me back for being so sloppy. What happened? Why did you change?"

Drew felt utterly disoriented now. None of this made any sense.

Maybe I'm dreaming, she thought.

Yes, that was probably what was going on. But she didn't like this dream very much, and she was ready to wake up.

He stepped forward and touched the back of the chair on the opposite side of the table from her.

"These are nice chairs," he said. "Where did you get them?"

Drew almost blurted that she'd bought them at a thrift shop. But what business was that of his? And if this was a dream, why didn't she just wake up?

The man ran his finger across the back of the chair and said, "Never mind. I know where *this* one came from. I've missed it. It's good to see it again."

Drew's head felt like it would explode with confusion.

She said in a shaky voice, "I think you'd better leave."

The man looked at her with an expression of genuine hurt.

"You're not happy to see me," he said. "You're surprised. I understand that. It's a shock. Things were ... so wrong when we last saw each other. But really, this is a good thing. I'm sure you'll feel the same way I do when you get used to it."

He took another step toward her.

She gestured sharply and said, "You've made a mistake. I'm not whoever you think I am."

"Not Mo?"

"No, I'm not. You'd better leave. I'll scream for help."

She took one step back, but he was suddenly upon her, gripping her by the hair. Her head slammed against something hard and her knees buckled.

She opened her mouth, but no sound came out.

Drew was barely conscious of his pushing the apartment door shut, bending over her, pulling her head back, and staring down into her face.

She heard his genuinely soothing voice, "I don't mean you any harm. I promise."

And the most terrifying thing of all was how sincere he looked and sounded, as if he wasn't doing anything wrong, as if he meant her nothing but kindness.

Then he held the sharp point of a knife against her throat.

"I'd never, ever hurt you," he said. "I promise."

The last thing Drew Cadigan felt was the blade plunging into her windpipe.

CHAPTER SEVEN

Riley felt an unsettling twinge when she and Jenn walked into the front hallway of Westminster Presbyterian Church. She often got this feeling on those rare occasions when she stepped inside a church—a peculiar sense of guilt.

She knew it made no sense for her to feel that way, but churches were such wholesome places, and Riley felt as though she really didn't belong inside them. After all, she spent her whole professional life immersed in the evil side of human nature.

For some irrational reason, she always felt as if she was bringing some kind of infection into a place of comfort and community. *Like evil might be catching.*

She knew she'd feel better when she got out of here.

Meanwhile, the hallway echoed with the sound of organ music coming from the nearby sanctuary.

Riley heard Jenn say, "'Nearer, My God, to Thee.'"

"Huh?" Riley said, looking at her.

"That's what the hymn is, in case you didn't know," Jenn said.

"I didn't know," Riley said.

Jenn shrugged and said, "Aunt Cora made us go to church from time to time."

Riley was startled. She was about to ask Jenn why her criminal foster parent would ever take her kids to church, but then she realized, *It was part of their training.*

They'd gone there to learn more about the perfectly innocent and ordinary sorts of people who would become the targets of their crimes.

It was a chilling thought—and ironic, too. Because of the criminal training Jenn had received from Aunt Cora, she was now probably more comfortable inside a church than Riley was.

Riley and Jenn walked into the church's main office and introduced themselves to the receptionist.

"Oh, yes," the woman said with a pleasant smile. "Buddy's expecting you. He's in the community hall, reorganizing things after an AA meeting. I'll take you there."

The woman led Riley and Jenn a short way down the hallway to a square room that was spacious enough to be used for banquets and other public gatherings. Chairs and tables were folded along the walls. The afternoon sunlight slanted in through a row of large windows and reflected off the hardwood floors.

A man was picking up folding chairs that had been arranged in a circle. The receptionist introduced him as Buddy Sears, a deacon at the church who served as its activity director. Sears invited Riley and Jenn to sit down with him on some of the remaining chairs.

Buddy Sears was a perfectly unremarkable-looking man with a small chin and a toothy smile and black-rimmed glasses. He folded his hands in his lap and looked back and forth between Riley and Jenn.

He said, "You mentioned on the phone that your visit has something to do with Joan Cornell. I've known her for years. I do hope nothing bad has happened to her."

Riley took a deep, slow breath, then said, "Mr. Sears—"

"Buddy, please," he said, gently interrupting.

Riley continued, "Buddy, my partner and I are sorry to be the ones to tell you this. But Joan Cornell was murdered in her home yesterday."

Buddy's mouth dropped open and he turned pale.

Jenn added, "We're hoping you can help us investigate her murder."

Buddy was shaking a little now. Riley was afraid he was going into shock and wouldn't be able to give lucid answers to their questions. She'd seen it happen to other people when she'd told them that someone they knew had died.

But Buddy seemed to gather his wits. After a long moment, he said, "Of course. I want to help in any way I can."

Riley said, "What can you tell me about your own relationship with the deceased?"

"Well, like I said, I've known her for a long time," Buddy said. "She and her husband, Thomas, were already regular churchgoers here when my family and I first moved into this neighborhood some twenty years ago. They really helped make us feel at home in Springett."

He shuffled his feet and continued, "But then a couple of years ago their marriage broke up, and Thomas moved away—up north to Maine, I believe. It was a shock to everybody here. Thomas and Joan and their kids always seemed like such a perfect family. But it sometimes happens like that when a couple's kids grow up and move far away. When the nest is empty, sometimes there's nothing left to hold a marriage together."

Riley felt a pang at those words. Her own marriage to Ryan had ended long before the two of them could become empty nesters. At least Thomas and Joan Cornell had lasted long enough for their children to be out on their own.

Then Buddy said, "Poor Joan sort of withdrew from the world for a while. As a deacon here at Westminster, and also as a friend, I spent a lot of time talking to her, trying to help her through it. Just recently, I thought maybe she was making some progress toward putting it all behind her. She was becoming more outgoing again, coming to our bingo games every week and showing up more often at church services. But now..."

His voice faded away.

In a gentle tone, Riley said, "Buddy, I know this is an awful thing to have to hear, but we're afraid whoever murdered Joan also killed somebody else a couple of weeks ago. Did you happen to know a man named Justin Selves?"

Jenn added, "He lived over in Petersboro. He probably wasn't a regular parishioner."

Buddy shook his head and said, "I don't believe I recognize the name."

Riley took out her computer pad and brought up a photo of Justin Selves. She showed it to Buddy and said, "We think he may have come to some of your bingo games. Does his face look familiar?"

Buddy squinted at the picture.

"No, but I'm terrible with faces. And besides, I'm busy making the bingo calls during our games, so I don't always notice who's here and who's not."

Riley glanced around at the room. It was obvious to her that the games were played right here. It was easy to imagine it with rows of tables filled with happy people playing bingo while Buddy made the calls over a sound system. Riley guessed that a hundred people might play here on any given Friday night. A single face could easily disappear among the crowd.

Buddy added, "We do have people from outside our church dropping in for our games, just to socialize and get to know people. He might have been one of those ..."

Then he looked back and forth at Riley and Jenn and said, "I think I know just the person who can help with this. Come with me."

Riley and Jenn followed Buddy out of the community room back into the hallway, where they could hear another hymn echoing through the air. Riley didn't recognize this one either, but she guessed Jenn probably did.

As they walked along, Buddy said, "Wanda Pettway has been the church organist for decades. She's got eyes like a hawk and never misses anything that goes on around here. She also helps with our bingo games every week—encourages the players and pretty much single-handedly keeps everything running. If the man you're talking about ever came to our games, she'd definitely recognize his face."

The organ music was almost painfully loud by the time they reached the Gothic-style sanctuary, a large chamber with stained glass windows. Riley guessed the woman at the organ didn't play at this volume during actual church services. Parishioners would be deafened if she did. Right now she must be enjoying having the sanctuary to herself and playing as loudly as she liked.

Buddy called out in the same sharp, clear voice Riley knew he must use when calling out bingo games, "Wanda!"

He had to yell her name a couple more times until the music stopped. The sudden silence was startling.

An elderly woman with a mane of orange-dyed hair looked out from behind the keyboard. She was wearing huge glasses with plastic gemstones on their frames.

"What is it, Buddy?" she asked.

"I'm afraid I've got some serious news," Buddy said. "Come and sit down with us."

The colorful woman got up from her bench and came down to join them. Wanda Pettway seemed to Riley like much too tiny a woman to play such a gigantic instrument, except for her exceptionally large hands and feet.

Buddy and Wanda sat down in the front pew together. Riley and Jenn stood facing them near the altar.

Buddy patted Wanda's hand and said, "These are two ladies are from the FBI—Agents Paige and Roston."

Wanda's eyes widened.

"Goodness!" she said. "What has happened? Was somebody murdered?"

"I'm afraid so," Buddy said. "Joan Cornell was found dead in her home yesterday."

"Oh, the poor dear!" Wanda said with a sigh.

She didn't seem especially shocked. Riley thought Wanda sounded as though she'd just been told been told somebody's pet had died.

Then Wanda's expression became sharply inquisitive.

"Tell me—do you know who did it? How was she killed?"

Jenn said, "We'd rather not get into specifics about the nature of her death."

Wanda nodded firmly and said, "Of course. Forgive me for asking. Procedure is everything in your line of work, isn't it?"

Riley couldn't help thinking the woman must have watched too many TV mysteries to grasp the reality of what had happened.

Then, with an eager expression on her face, the church organist leaned toward Jenn and Riley.

She said, "If you're looking for the killer, I think I know who it was!"

CHAPTER EIGHT

Riley felt a jolt of surprise. She certainly hadn't expected the church organist to say anything like this.

She wondered, *Could it be true? Could this woman know the man we're looking for?*

"Please explain," Jenn said to Wanda.

"Well," Wanda began in a self-satisfied tone, "there was this fellow who sometimes comes to our bingo games. Not a parishioner, but he comes to our games most Fridays. I think he's divorced. He had kind of a thing for Joan. He'd always sit beside her at the bingo table and flirt with her during the games."

Wanda added in a conspiratorial whisper, "I could tell she didn't like him at all. And he really wasn't very attractive, if you want to know what I think."

"Do you know his name?" Riley asked.

"Of course, Wanda said, "His name is Tony Moore."

Riley glanced at Buddy, who just shrugged.

Then the organist continued, "One night—some two or three Fridays ago, I think—Tony got way too pushy. When he arrived at the table, two people were already seated in the chairs on either side of Joan, and he couldn't plop himself down and make a nuisance of himself to her like he usually did."

She let out a huff of disapproval.

"So Tony talked the woman to Joan's right into switching chairs so he could sit next to Joan. Well, anyone could see that Joan had finally had enough of him. She got up and walked straight out of the community room, heading for the front door. And in just a few seconds, Tony got up and walked out too."

With a click of her tongue, Wanda said, "I didn't like the looks of that. I was worried about what Tony might do if he caught Joan by herself. So I went right after him, just to make sure he didn't bother her."

Wanda glanced around the group, as if to make sure her audience was paying attention, then she continued, "Tony followed Joan on out through the front door. So I stood there in the doorway with the door cracked so I could see and hear what was happening outside."

Wanda shook her head.

"Things were really getting ugly. Joan had gotten into her car and was ready to drive off, but Tony was standing there holding her car door open and leaning in toward her so she couldn't leave. He kept telling her that he knew she liked him more than she let on, and he was getting tired of her teasing him along like this, and he said he wasn't going to budge until she agreed to go out with him."

Wanda shrugged.

"I felt like I should do something, but I didn't know what. Tony's a strong guy, and I was afraid to get in the middle of things. I didn't want to get hurt."

Buddy put in, "You should have come and told me, Wanda. I could have helped. I had no idea that anything like that was going on."

"Well, I think maybe I was getting ready to come and get you," Wanda said. "But it wasn't necessary, as it turned out. There was another man out there—a bingo player who'd stepped out for a cigarette. He walked over to the car and asked Joan if the man was giving her any trouble."

"Then what happened?" Jenn asked.

"Tony told the man to mind his own business, but the man shoved him away from the car. Tony raised up his fists like he was fixing for a fight, but he seemed to think better of it. The other man was taller and looked like he was in better shape than Tony, and it was pretty clear that Tony would probably have gotten the worst of it. So Tony just cursed and stomped over to his own car and drove off. Joan thanked the man and she drove away too." Wanda added sadly, "Poor Joan."

"What about the man?" Buddy asked.

"He kind of stood there frowning for a moment, looking like his evening was pretty much spoiled, and then he went to his car and drove away too. That was the last I saw of any of them. None of them have come to our games since."

Wanda craned her head toward Jenn and Riley.

She said, "And now you're telling me poor Joan was murdered. And I'll bet anything Tony did it. And all because she didn't want to have anything to do with him. Don't you think so too?"

Neither Riley nor Jenn replied. Riley was beginning to consider Tony a very likely suspect, but she wasn't ready to say so. Besides, she didn't want to express any agreement with this rather annoying woman.

Jenn said to Wanda, "What about the man who pushed him? What can you tell us about him?"

Wanda tilted her head in thought.

"Not much, to tell you the truth. He wasn't a parishioner, but he came to our bingo games several times. He was a nice man, very polite and outgoing, and I'd always meant to introduce myself to him, but I never caught his name. I'm sure some of the other players must have known him."

Riley felt a tingle of anticipation as she remembered what she and Jenn had come to ask Wanda in the first place. She took out her computer pad and brought up the photo she had of Justin Selves.

She said to Wanda, "Does this face look familiar?"

Wanda's mouth dropped open.

"Why, it's him! It's the man who stopped Tony from pestering Joan!"

Then she knitted her brow and added, "Why are you showing me this? What does he have to do with the murder?"

Riley would have been just as happy not to answer Wanda's question.

But Buddy said, "He was murdered too, Wanda. He was killed a couple of weeks ago."

Wanda gasped and said, "How awful! And it must have been Tony who did it! So he actually murdered two people!"

Riley was finding it more and more likely that Wanda was right.

Jenn asked Buddy, "Do you happen to know Tony Moore?"

Buddy shook his head. "I'm afraid not. I must have seen him here at the games, but I never took notice of him. Like I said, I was busy calling the games."

Riley asked Wanda, "What else can you tell me about Tony Moore?"

"Not much, but I *can* tell you where he works," Wanda said pertly. "I see him when I shop at LangMart, usually in the afternoons. I run into him in the aisles there, and he's always wearing the company uniform. I say hello to him, just to be polite. But he pretends not to know me. He's not a nice man. I'm not surprised that he's also a killer."

Riley and Jenn looked at each other and exchanged nods. Riley knew she and her partner were both thinking the same thing. They thanked Wanda and Buddy for their time and help, asked them not to discuss the case with anyone, then left the church.

As they walked toward the car, Jenn said, "It's him. Tony Moore is our killer."

"He might well be," Riley said. "We need to pay him a visit."

They got into the car. Before starting the engine, Riley used her cell phone to try to track down either Tony Moore's address or phone number. But there were four people by that name right here in Springett.

Riley grumbled, "I guess I'll have to call them one by one until I get the right one."

"Not necessarily," Jenn said. "Remember, Wanda said that he works at LangMart in the afternoons. He could be at work right now."

"You're right," Riley said. "Let's head on over there."

Jenn found the address for LangMart, and Riley drove following her directions.

On the way, Riley thought about what they'd just learned.

A man named Tony Moore had quarreled with two people just outside Westminster Presbyterian Church some three weeks ago.

And both of those people wound up dead.

Of course, Riley knew that the connection might be coincidental. But what if Tony Moore really was the killer they were looking for?

He'd probably been motivated from sheer spite toward a woman who wouldn't go out with him, and also toward a man who had stood up to him on the woman's behalf. He might be a terrible man, but he wasn't driven by some psychotic urge to kill again and again.

If so, Riley realized, *Jenn might have been right from the very beginning.*

They weren't hunting a serial killer after all.

CHAPTER NINE

When Riley and Jenn walked into LangMart, Riley's eyes darted uneasily around the hypermarket. They were looking for a man who might have murdered two people because they'd angered him. The last thing she wanted was to get him agitated in this vast maze of aisles full of every conceivable kind of merchandise and cluttered with shoppers. If Tony Moore was here, how were they going to corner him?

She said to Jenn, "We've got to be careful. Let's not advertise our presence."

Jenn nodded and said, "Right. He could easily slip away from us in a place like this."

They found the customer service counter and asked a female employee if they could speak to the store's manager.

Looking understandably concerned, she said, "Um, are you sure it's something I can't help you with? My job is to keep customers happy. If you've got a complaint or want to return something—"

Riley gently interrupted, "It's nothing like that. We just need to see the manager."

The woman nodded warily, then called over the intercom for the manager to come to customer service. Soon a hearty-looking man came trotting up to the counter. His name tag read WAYNE.

The employee said to him, "These ladies said they'd like to talk to you."

With a professional smile, Wayne said to Riley and Jenn, "How may I help you?"

Neither Riley nor Jenn took out their badges. Riley hoped that wouldn't be necessary.

Riley said to him, "We're looking for an employee of yours named Tony Moore."

Wayne's smile faded as if this wasn't quite unexpected.

"Oh, no," he said. "Do you wish to make a complaint against him? Has he done something to bother you?"

Jenn said, "No, we just want to talk with him."

Wayne squinted at them curiously.

He said, "You seem like a couple of nice ladies. Are you friends of his?"

Riley exchanged glances with Jenn.

Then Riley said, "Could we step behind the counter with you for a moment?"

"Of course," Wayne said.

He opened a half-door, and Riley and Jenn followed him behind the counter. They discreetly took out their badges and showed them to him.

Riley said quietly, "I'm Special Agent Riley Paige with the FBI, and this is my partner, Special Agent Roston. We really need to speak to Tony Moore if that's at all possible."

Wayne's expression darkened.

"Good God," he muttered, his professional demeanor suddenly gone. "I should have figured. What the hell did that bastard do?"

Riley noted the tone of dislike in the manager's voice.

Jenn said, "We're not accusing him of anything. And we'd rather not get into details. We just need to talk to him."

"I think I know where we can find him," Wayne said. "Come with me."

As they strode together through the aisles, the manager added, "I should have fired that guy weeks ago."

"Has he been a problem?" Riley asked.

"He's been nothing but problems. Customers complain about him all the time. Especially women. And he's completely unreliable, comes and goes whenever he likes. He disappeared for a couple of hours just this afternoon, then showed up a little while ago without offering any explanation. Should have cut him loose right then, but it can be hard to get good people for this kind of work."

Probably hard because of the wages paid here, Riley thought. But she just nodded and made no comment.

Wayne led the two agents all the way to the back of the store. From there they passed through a door marked EMPLOYEES ONLY into a huge stock room the size of a small warehouse.

Wayne called out, "Moore, are you in here somewhere?"

A voice echoed back, "Right here, boss."

They followed the voice into an aisle flanked by metal shelves filled with packaged merchandise. A man in his fifties was standing beside a long dolly that was piled high with boxes, unloading the boxes onto the shelves.

"What do you want?" the man asked gruffly.

Riley and Jenn produced their badges again, but before they could introduce themselves, the man yelped out, "Oh, shit."

He gave the dolly a hard shove.

Before Riley and Jenn could react, boxes were falling around them as the dolly crashed into a shelf. Both Wayne and Jenn were knocked down, and Riley had to scramble to regain her footing.

Now anger drove Riley as she clambered over the fallen boxes and launched herself forward, tackling Tony as he turned to run away.

He struggled as they rolled about on the floor and Riley found him surprisingly hard to hold onto. He wriggled clear of her grasp and made it to his feet.

Riley grabbed an ankle, and the man tumbled down again. She scrambled over to him and slammed her fist into his face. The man moaned and went limp, clearly giving up the fight.

Riley stood up and lifted him roughly to his feet. He stared at her with his eyes all bloodshot and his breath smelling of alcohol.

Suddenly, she felt a surge of inexplicable rage.

It was as if she had no idea where she was or what she was doing.

She punched the man in the stomach, and he buckled over with a loud gasp of shock and pain.

She was about to hit him again when she heard Jenn's voice. "Riley, stop it!"

Riley unclenched her fist and took a deep breath to calm herself.

She whipped out her handcuffs and said, "Tony Moore, you're under arrest for assaulting a law enforcement officer and resisting arrest."

She read him his rights as she put the cuffs on him.

As they led the man away past the dumbfounded manager, Jenn whispered to Riley, "What the hell were you doing just now? What were you thinking?"

Riley didn't reply, but she knew the answer to Jenn's question.

She had kept hitting him because it felt good to do that, as though she'd been striking back at a multitude of frustrations in her life.

⚜   ⚜   ⚜

A little while later, Riley and Jenn were in an interrogation room at the Springett police station facing Tony Moore, who was seated at a gray table in handcuffs.

"Where's my lawyer?" Tony said.

"He'll be here soon," Jenn said.

Riley knew that was true. As soon as they'd brought Tony into the station and he had asked for a lawyer, Chief Shore had put in a phone call for a public defender. But Shore had assured Riley and Jenn that the lawyer wouldn't arrive in any great hurry. Riley hoped that maybe they could make good use of the time before he showed up.

She and Jenn were pacing in front of the table, hoping to make Tony uncomfortable with their restless movements. Riley eyed the man closely, remembering her unexpected burst of fury toward him back in the stockroom.

It had felt good to take him down, but she knew that in hitting him that last time she had gone beyond the exhilaration of capturing a criminal. It had felt cathartic.

She probably wouldn't have stopped if Jenn hadn't yelled at her.

After a couple of decades as a BAU agent, why had she lapsed into such unprofessional behavior?

What had stressed her out so much that she had needed that catharsis?

She knew part of it must be because of Blaine breaking up with her. After all the time they had enjoyed together, after he had pushed for ways to spend even more time together, it had seemed so unfair that he could just walk in and end things like that. She had come to trust him, to believe that he wanted them to be together, that they would somehow work things out.

Of course, she admitted to herself, Blaine had been right. She wouldn't have ended the relationship like that, but it was always doomed to end. He would never have adjusted to her lifestyle, just as her ex-husband had never adjusted to her lifestyle. They both made her furious, all the more so because she knew they were both right.

Now that her repressed aggression had come out at last, Riley felt ashamed that she'd let it get the best of her.

She was glad that Jenn had snapped her out of it before she could hit the man again. But shame wasn't all that Riley felt as she recalled that moment. She was disturbed by her own actions and she knew that there was more to her frustration than just Blaine leaving.

Maybe it's a sign of getting old, she thought.

Maybe it really was time for her to get into a different line of work.

These struck her as strange thoughts to be having while she was gearing up to interview a potential murder suspect. In fact, the whole situation was beginning to seem weirdly ironic.

For years and years, she'd blamed herself and been blamed by her loved ones for bringing the ugliness and violence of her work into her home life. And now, for some reason, she was bringing her home life into her work.

It's time to cut it out, she thought.

After all, she had to take advantage of the opportunity she had right now. Tony Moore's behavior was so suspicious that he seemed almost like a gift from heaven. The simple fact that he'd tried to run away from them indicated that he was guilty of something.

Riley paused in her pacing and said to Moore in a mock-kindly voice, "This is kind of tedious, isn't it? Just waiting here like this. We're sorry about that. What do you say we chat a little to pass the time?"

Taking Riley's lead, Jenn added in a similar tone, "Yeah, why don't we? My partner and I don't know anything about you, Tony Moore. We'd like to get to know you better."

Moore's eyes darted back and forth between them.

"Like how?" he said.

Riley felt a twinge of encouragement. Instead of insisting on clamming up until his lawyer arrived, he was opening himself up just a crack to conversation. Maybe Riley and Jenn would get something out of him before the lawyer got here.

Riley sat casually on the edge of the table.

"Well, maybe you could tell us a few things about yourself," she said. "Like, what do you like to do in your spare time? What are your favorite games?"

"What kind of games?" Tony asked.

"Any kind of games," Jenn said. "Board games, maybe."

"I don't know," Tony said with a shrug. "I used to play checkers when I was a kid."

"Chess?" Riley asked.

Tony scoffed and said, "Naw, that one's too hard for me. Monopoly some. Not so much anymore."

"How about bingo?" Jenn asked.

Tony's eyes widened with interest.

"Bingo, sure. I like that a lot."

Riley couldn't help but smile.

Bingo, indeed!

71

He certainly wasn't being secretive. If she and Jenn played their cards skillfully enough, he'd tell them everything they wanted to know. The man wasn't at all bright.

Definitely not a chess player.

Judging from his breath and bloodshot eyes and the slight slur of his words, he also wasn't entirely sober.

Those factors might make questioning quite easy.

"Where do you play bingo?" Riley asked.

Tony smiled as if he was starting to enjoy this little chat.

He said, "Well, I *did* like to play Friday nights over at Westminster Presbyterian Church."

"Are you a religious man?" Jenn asked.

"Naw, but they run a good bingo game. Nice prizes. You get to meet lots of nice people there."

"Including nice women?" Riley asked.

Tony chuckled and said, "Sure, that's part of the idea of going. It's hard to meet nice women when you get to be my age."

"You're not married, I take it," Jenn said.

"No, I'm between marriages, you might say. Been married four times."

Riley got up from the table and said, "Trouble with relationships?"

"Yeah, but it's not because of me," Tony said. "It's always the women. I keep picking the wrong girl somehow. Haven't met the right one yet."

Jenn crossed her arms and said, "Have you got your eye on one these days? At the bingo games, I mean?"

He grunted slightly and said, "I can't say I do."

Riley and Jenn looked at each other with mock surprise.

"No?" Jenn said. "Are you sure of that?"

Riley added, "We'd heard otherwise."

"I don't know what you're talking about," Tony said.

Jenn leaned across the table and said, "We hear that you'd been putting the moves on an attractive divorcée named Joan Cornell."

Tony's eyes widened with surprise.

"Who told you that?" he said.

"Word gets around," Riley said.

"Well, it's not true," Tony said.

Jenny craned closer to him and said, "Not true that you were interested in Joan?"

Tony shrugged.

"OK, I was interested in her for a while. But I lost interest. As a matter of fact, I lost interest in the whole game thing there at Westminster. I'm not going there anymore. I'm looking to find another game at another church."

Tony glanced around with a worried expression.

"What's this all about anyway?" he said. "What did you even arrest me for?"

Riley said, "We told you back at LangMart when we put the cuffs on you. You assaulted and resisted an officer of the law."

Tony glared at Riley and said, "You punched me."

"Only after you assaulted us," Riley said. "You pushed a dolly full of boxes at us. You knocked down my partner and your boss too. Isn't that correct?"

Tony wrinkled his brow in thought for a moment, then nodded. Riley felt relieved that he was apparently too stupid to comprehend that she'd used unnecessary force.

On the other hand, she wondered, was his stupidity just an act?

He might be smarter than he looks, she thought.

In any case, she felt as though it was time to get right to the point.

She said, "I think you know why we're asking about your relationship with Joan Cornell."

"No, I've got no idea," he said.

Jenn put in, "Oh, I think you do."

"No, really, I don't," he said.

"Joan Cornell was murdered yesterday," Riley said.

Tony inhaled sharply.

"Huh?" he said.

Jenn added, "And a couple of weeks ago, a man was murdered the same way she was. His name was Justin Selves. You knew him too, didn't you?"

"Never heard of him," Tony said.

"No?" Jenn said.

"That's odd," Riley added. "Because we have a witness who saw you have an altercation with Selves just outside the church the last night you were there. He didn't like how you were treating Joan, the witness said. And Joan didn't like it either. Selves pushed you away from her car."

Tony's mouth was hanging open now.

Jenn said, "Are you going to tell us it's just a coincidence that the two people you quarreled with that night wound up dead?"

Suddenly sounding quite sober, Tony said, "I'm not telling you anything. Not without a lawyer."

But Riley felt as though she was just getting started.

He'll talk, all right.

But before either she or Jenn could ask another question, the door to the interrogation room opened and Chief Shore poked his head inside.

He said, "Agents Paige and Roston, I need to have a word with you."

Riley didn't like having the flow of the interview interrupted. Nevertheless, she and Jenn both stepped out into the hallway.

Then Chief Shore told them, "There's been another murder."

CHAPTER TEN

Riley felt a jolt of despair. Everything had just changed.

She heard Jenn, who was standing beside her in the police station hallway, mutter, "Oh, Christ."

Riley had actually started to hope that Jenn was right after all—that the murders of Joan Cornell and Justin Selves were not the work of a serial killer. Their interview with Tony Moore had made it seem possible that he had killed them in a simple pique of anger over what had happened outside that church on bingo night.

Now the killer had struck again, and the likelihood of it being a simple argument faded away. Riley listened as Chief Shore described exactly the same MO as the earlier murders. This was a serial, and whether it was Moore or someone else, they had failed to stop him in time to save a life.

Riley asked Chief Shore, "When did it happen? And where?"

Chief Shore said, "Just a little while ago, over in an apartment house near the Springett College campus. It was a college student this time. Her roommate, Sylvia Jaffe, found her body just a few minutes ago. The county coroner's on his way there as we speak. I'm going to drive over there right now."

"We'll follow you in our car," Riley said.

As the three of them headed down the hall to leave the building, Shore added, "There's one more thing you should know. Earlier I told you that some of my guys were examining Moore's car for evidence. So far they haven't found anything linking Moore to the two murders. But they did find out that his car matches the description of a vehicle involved in a hit and run accident the day before yesterday. There's even a dent in the front bumper that looks like where the victim was probably hit."

Riley felt another jolt of surprise. Suddenly, everything seemed much more complicated.

Riley and Jenn got into their borrowed car and followed the chief through the streets of Springett.

"Another murder," Riley muttered, shaking her head as she drove.

Jenn said, "Yeah, but that sure doesn't rule Moore out as a suspect. Remember what his boss said—that he'd disappeared from work for a couple of hours a little while ago. Somebody will have to check and see what kind of an alibi he's got, if any."

Riley didn't reply, but she knew Jenn was right. Moore was still a viable suspect for the time being. Still, she was feeling less and less certain of it.

Jenn added, "This hit and run thing is an odd development."

"More than odd," Riley said. "It's another complication."

"What do you mean?" Jenn asked.

Stifling a sigh, Riley said, "Think about it, Jenn. He tried to run away from us back at that LangMart store. We've been assuming it's because of his guilt over the murders. But maybe we're wrong."

"You mean ...?"

Riley said, "I mean maybe he tried to get away because he thought we were after him for the hit and run. Maybe he had no idea about the murders."

Jenn scoffed. "Oh, come on, Riley."

"It's a possibility," Riley said.

Jenn said, "Just because he's guilty of a hit and run doesn't mean he didn't also commit the two murders. In fact, I'm not sure it doesn't make him an even more likely suspect, a certified sociopath. Are you seriously trying to tell me that he just happened to argue that night with the two people who wound up dead?"

Riley didn't reply, but she thought, *Yeah, that's exactly what I'm trying to tell you.*

She'd learned years ago—and had tried to teach Jenn—that coincidences were an inevitable part of investigative work. If Tony Moore hadn't committed the two murders after all, it would be far from the strangest coincidence she'd encountered during her career as a BAU agent.

Nevertheless, Riley hoped that her worries were for nothing, and that the culprit of all three of the murders was now safely in custody.

Riley pulled behind Chief Shore's vehicle as he parked in front of a three-story, wood-framed house. The neighborhood looked like it had once been fairly prosperous, but had since gone somewhat to seed.

Some police cars and the coroner's van were already parked outside the house. A handful of cops was keeping a crowd of gawking neighbors away from the front door. Riley was relieved not to see any sign of reporters just yet.

But it's only a matter of time.

So far, all the media knew about the case was that two separate murders had taken place in two neighboring suburbs of Philadelphia. In a city this size, that wasn't going to attract immediate attention. The cops had been careful to keep details quiet, so reporters hadn't yet caught on that there was any connection between them.

Riley knew this new killing was likely to change that.

She, Jenn, and Chief Shore got out of their vehicles and walked up toward the house.

Chief Shore called out to one of the cops, "Show us the crime scene."

Riley, Jenn, and Shore followed the cop onto the wide front porch and through the front door. In the front room were gathered about nine terrified-looking young people—the victim's housemates, Riley was sure. She and Jenn flashed their badges at them, and they nodded mutely.

We'll need to talk to them later, Riley thought.

The cop led Riley, Jenn, and Chief Shore a short way down the hall to one of the apartments.

The coroner and one white-uniformed assistant were crouched over a young woman's body, which lay crumpled on the floor. For some reason, Riley found herself trying not to look straight at the victim. Even so, she saw that quite a lot of blood had spread on the room's cheap flooring.

"Who was she?" Chief Shore asked the cop who had brought them here.

The cop said, "Her name was Drew Cadigan, and she was a sophomore here at Springett College. Her roommate came in and found her a little while ago."

Riley asked, "Where's her roommate right now?"

"She's in pretty bad shape," the cop said. "She's sitting on the back stoop by herself."

Chief Shore said, "Go make sure that neither she nor any of the other kids leave the premises."

The cop nodded and headed back down the hallway.

Her eyes still avoiding the body, Riley glanced around the place. It looked like a pretty ordinary student apartment, with two bed-rooms and a bathroom and a small kitchen area. It reminded Riley of places where she and Ryan had lived together early on, except that it was much more cluttered and untidy.

On a small table at one end of the kitchen area was an open carton of melting ice cream with a tablespoon dipped into it. Riley figured the poor woman must have been snacking when she was attacked. Riley also noticed that there was just one straight-backed chair at the little table where she must have been sitting.

Looks like another chair is missing, she thought.

The coroner got to his feet, and Riley and Jenn showed him their badges.

Chief Shore said to Riley and Jenn, "Agents Paige and Roston, this is Tyler Broadhurst, the county coroner. He's been to the other two crime scenes."

The short, stubby coroner nodded and added, "Yeah, and I did autopsies on both of those victims. I can't say I like the looks of this one."

"What do you mean?" Jenn asked.

"Her eyes are still open," Broadhurst said, pointing to the victim's face.

Riley still avoided looking at it directly.

What's the matter with me? she wondered.

She'd long since been hardened to the sight of dead bodies.

Why did this one seem to be different?

Broadhurst continued explaining, "Just like he did with the others, the killer tried to knock her out cold by hitting her head here."

He pointed to a bloody mark on one side of the table.

"But he didn't quite succeed," he added. "Which means she was still conscious when he cut her throat. She knew exactly what was happening to her. She was in pain, too, from the blow to her head. Damn, but I do hate these ugly cases."

Riley could tell by his tone that these three killings were far from the first murders he'd dealt with. As the official coroner for this whole county, that was hardly surprising. Still, she wondered just how many serial killings he'd worked on during his career.

This one might be tough even for him, she thought.

"Leave me alone to move around the crime scene," she said to the others in the room.

Broadhurst, his assistant, and Chief Shore looked a bit surprised at the request.

But Jenn obviously understood exactly what Riley had in mind.

"Let's just do as she says," Jenn said to the three men in the room.

Jenn led them out the door, and Riley crouched beside the body, hoping to get some sense of the killer's mind.

And now, at last, she looked the victim straight in the face.

Although she was usually numb to even the most horrific sights, she was startled to feel a wave of horror and revulsion that she seldom experienced anymore. She quickly realized why. She'd experienced a chill of déjà vu back when she'd seen photos of the other two victims, but now…

I'm having a flashback.

And it was really powerful and unnerving.

CHAPTER ELEVEN

When Riley arrived at her dorm room that morning, she found that the door was already open just a crack.

She felt a wave of alarm.

Something's wrong, *she thought.*

She stood frozen for a long moment.

She called to her roommate through the door.

"Trudy?"

No answer came.

Riley pushed the door open.

She clicked on the light.

Blood was everywhere.

When she saw Trudy lying amidst the blood with her throat slashed, Riley started screaming.

She screamed so loudly that everyone in the dorm must have heard her.

Trying to calm herself, Riley struggled to think of what do.

Try to stop the bleeding? *she thought.*

What good would it do? It looked like Trudy wasn't bleeding anymore. And if she wasn't bleeding, that meant she must be dead.

Even so, Riley yelled at Trudy and shook her. She tried to perform CPR, pressing down on Trudy's chest, but she had to stop when blood started to bubble from the wound again.

Riley shuddered deeply as she relived that horrible moment. It has been long ago, back when she was in college. Now the sight of this victim, Drew Cadigan, had set off that memory. The murdered girl looked uncannily like Trudy had when Riley had found her dead, lying in her own blood, with the same horrified expression on her face.

Riley struggled to catch her breath.

That long-ago ordeal felt as though it were happening right now.

Trudy had been the third murder victim Riley had seen in her whole life. The first had been her own mother, when Riley was just a child. Then Trudy's murder and that of another college friend had propelled her into a career in the FBI.

And now, at this moment, she was strangely lightheaded, as though that whole career was about to flash before her eyes.

Remember what you're here to do, she told herself.

She snapped herself out of her flashback and looked hard at the victim.

She hoped her instincts would kick in better than they had earlier. Joan Cornell's body had been gone when Riley and Jenn had been at that murder scene earlier today. Although Riley was sometimes able to get a sense of a killer even after a scene had been cleaned up, she'd picked up nothing at all there.

But now she and Jenn had been able to arrive at the murder scene much sooner than was usually possible. Everything was remarkably undisturbed. The body was still here—and freshly slain.

Maybe, in spite of her personal reaction of horror, it would be easier for her to slip into the killer's mind here and now.

Or maybe even because *of the flashback,* she thought grimly.

Even after all these years as a successful agent, she couldn't explain exactly how her ability to sense a killer's mind worked. She knew it was partly based on actual clues and partly pure imagination. But she had learned that, however vague the experience might be, it could give her valuable insight into a crime.

She rose to her feet and walked outside in the doorway, standing where the killer must have stood just before he came in.

She breathed slowly and tried to imagine how things had unfolded from his point of view.

First of all she wondered—how had he managed to enter the apartment?

Maybe the door was open, she thought.

In a cozy apartment house like this, it was probably common for students not to bother locking their doors, and maybe even to leave them standing open during the day.

If so, the killer may have just walked inside without bothering to knock.

Riley stepped through the doorway into the room. She looked again at the open ice cream carton on the table. The tablespoon had sunk deeper into the gooey, rapidly melting ice cream just during the time since Riley and Jenn had arrived.

Riley realized the killer must have found Drew Cadigan right here digging into the ice cream.

Either celebrating something good or consoling herself for something bad.

Then he must have stood inside the doorway and said something to her.

Did she know him personally?

Somehow, Riley doubted it. Although the killer had undoubtedly chosen her in advance and might have been stalking her for some time, she'd probably never even spoken to him. Most likely, she had never even noticed him before.

And now, when he came in, he said something disarming and unthreatening to give her a false sense of security.

Like maybe to ask whether he'd come to the wrong apartment looking for somebody.

The girl might not have been alarmed at first, but then ...

He started walking toward her.

Riley stepped forward in what must have been his footsteps.

He kept talking, trying to keep her calm.

But how could Drew have helped sensing that something was very wrong with her visitor?

Surely she'd started feeling uneasy fairly quickly.

Still slowly walking toward the table, Riley realized something.

The chair.

The missing chair had been here then, probably directly across the table from where Drew had been sitting.

The chair had clearly mattered to the killer, since he'd apparently stolen it.

Did he say something to her about it?

Riley thought maybe he had—and that he'd maybe touched the chair at that moment. It must have seemed to Drew like weird talk and a weird gesture.

So she asked him to leave, but he wouldn't.

And then, when she'd risen from the table hoping to get away from him...

He was too fast for her.

He'd leaped forward, grabbed her by the hair, and slammed her head against the table. Had he looked into her eyes to see whether she'd lost consciousness? If he had, he apparently hadn't cared.

So he cut her throat.

Riley stood staring at the body, wondering, *Then what?*

Any sense of connection she'd gotten with the killer was suddenly gone. It hadn't been strong at all, and she felt discouraged. Still, the effort hadn't been totally wasted. She'd gotten the strong feeling that he had managed to seem unthreatening and maybe even a bit charming, at least when he first entered the room.

Again, Riley found herself remembering her two college friends who had been killed in much the same way. Their killer had turned out to be a popular and trusted person. Charming on the outside, but a stone-cold psychopath just beneath the skin.

Is this one like that? she wondered.

Maybe—or maybe not. Riley wasn't sure. But the missing pieces of furniture added a peculiar dimension to these killings. This certainly wouldn't be the first killer Riley had hunted who had taken souvenirs of his murders, oftentimes small personal items or pieces of clothing.

Those souvenirs usually indicated a sexual component to the killings. The killer took them to relive the gratification of the killing itself.

But chairs?

There was something weirdly different about these thefts—almost a kind of sick, misguided, and yet utterly nonsexual intimacy.

All Riley knew for sure was that this killer was different from any she'd ever dealt with in all her years with the BAU.

Riley called her colleagues back into the room. She said to the coroner and his assistant, "You can take the body away whenever you feel ready."

As the two men got to work preparing the body to be removed, Riley said to Jenn and Chief Shore, "I want you two to go back to the front room, start questioning the kids who live here to find out if they saw or heard anything. I'm going to talk to the roommate."

Jenn and Shore walked back toward the front of the house, and Riley went farther down the hall until she came to the back door. The door was open, and a young woman was sitting on a stoop just outside, staring out over the badly kept backyard.

A young policewoman was standing nearby, looking restless. Riley told her that she could join her team, and the woman hurried off.

Then Riley turned to the young woman sitting on the stoop, who gave no sign of noticing anything that was going on around her.

Riley swallowed hard.

Again, she remembered her own horror at finding the bodies of her two college friends. And now she had to talk to another college girl who had just experienced the same thing.

This isn't going to be easy, Riley thought.

Chapter Twelve

With a deep feeling of apprehension, Riley quietly sat down on the step beside the roommate of the murdered girl.

In a gentle voice, she said, "Sylvia—your name is Sylvia, isn't it?"

Still staring away, Sylvia silently nodded.

Riley took out her badge and said, "I'm Special Agent Riley Paige with the FBI."

Sylvia didn't look at the badge.

Riley said, "I'm terribly, terribly sorry about what happened."

Sylvia still didn't react.

Riley said, "I need to ask you some questions."

Still there was no reaction. It was as if Sylvia were unaware of Riley's presence.

Riley wasn't the least bit surprised.

The poor kid's still in shock, she thought.

She touched Sylvia gently on the shoulder and told her, "I'm going to say something you're not going to believe."

Riley paused, then added, "I know exactly what you're going through."

Sylvia's body lurched a little.

She said in a hoarse whisper, "You can't. That's ... impossible."

"It's true," Riley said. "What year are you in college?"

"A sophomore," Sylvia said.

Riley inhaled slowly and said, "Well, when I was a senior, not much older than you, I found two of my friends dead, killed in exactly the same way. One was my roommate. I found her in our room, just like you did."

Still not looking at Riley, Sylvia asked, "How...did you cope?"

Riley felt jolted by the question. How could she begin to answer it? The truth was, she was still coping with those traumas. Her whole career was at least partly about coming to terms with them.

As she tried to think of what to say, it occurred to Riley, *Why not the truth?*

Or at least part of the truth?

Choosing her words carefully, Riley said, "I tried to help. I did everything I could to help find my friends' killer."

"Did they ever catch him?" Sylvia asked.

"They did," Riley said, pushing back the memories of her own desperate struggle with the killer, and how she'd almost died during those awful moments before she'd been rescued and her attacker was arrested.

"I want to help," Sylvia said.

"Good," Riley said. "Now I need for you to remember the moments leading up to when you found Drew. You'd been out of the house, I take it."

Sylvia nodded. "I'd just gotten out of an anthropology class," she said.

"And you walked straight home from the campus?" Riley said.

"Yeah, I don't have a car. Neither did Drew."

Riley patted her on the shoulder.

"You're doing great, Sylvia. Now I need for you to think back to your walk. Did you run into anyone or even just see anyone on the way to the house?"

Squinting with thought, Sylvia said, "I ran into Rosaura and Faith, a couple of friends from some of my other classes. They wanted to know whether Drew and I wanted to get together with them at the Memorial Union later on. I said I'd like to come, and I'd ask Drew whether she wanted to come too."

"Go on," Riley said. "Did you notice any strangers?"

"I saw a few other students on the way, too. I didn't know some of their names, but their faces were familiar. I'd seen them before lots of times. None of them were total strangers."

"Who else did you see during your walk?" Riley asked.

Sylvia's wrinkled her brow.

"I saw … this old lady walking her fluffy little dog—a Pomeranian, I think. I don't know her name, but we see each other out walking a lot, and we always wave and smile at each other."

Riley was glad Sylvia seemed to be so observant. She'd interviewed way too many witnesses who didn't pay any attention to what was going on around them.

"Did you see anyone else on your way home?" Riley said.

Sylvia shook her head.

"No," she said. "Nobody else."

"Are you sure?"

"I'm sure."

Riley believed her.

"Tell me exactly what happened when you got to the house," Riley said.

"Well, I got out my key to open the front door to the house, but I noticed that the latch was taped so the door opened right up. It's been like that a lot lately. Some of our housemates keep putting tape on the latch so they or their friends don't have to worry about keys. Drew and I have been complaining about that, but it doesn't make any difference, they just keep doing it."

Riley noticed Sylvia's expression darken.

"They shouldn't have done that," she said. "If they hadn't done that…"

Sylvia's voice faded.

"What about when you came inside?" Riley asked.

"I heard music and talking in some of the other rooms," Sylvia said. "I guess most of my housemates were at home. But I didn't see anyone in the hall as I walked to our room."

Sylvia fell quiet for a moment, then said, "When I got to our room, the door was partly open. That's not unusual. We both leave it like that a lot. And then … I got a lot of impressions … really fast."

She tilted her head and continued, "The first thing I noticed was an open ice cream carton. Chocolate chip cookie dough, both of our favorite. It had a spoon in it and it was just sitting there on the table. We'd been saving it for some kind of celebration together, but there it was, open and starting to melt."

Sylvia shrugged slightly.

"I wasn't really mad, just kind of amused, but I thought I'd pretend to be mad just to tease her, so I got ready to yell about it, and then..."

Sylvia shuddered.

"Then I noticed that a chair wasn't where it was supposed to be, and when I glanced around for it, I saw her lying there on the other side of the table, and I thought she'd had some kind of accident, like maybe she'd fallen and gotten hurt. I said her name and when I walked over and bent down to shake her, I saw... the wound..."

Sylvia swallowed hard and stared off into space again.

Riley asked, "Did you call nine-one-one?"

"No, I just screamed a whole lot. I guess somebody else called nine-one-one. I should have handled things better. I'm feeling... so guilty."

"That's natural," Riley said. "I felt that way after I found my friend. But you've got nothing to feel guilty about. There was nothing you could do."

A single sob burst out of Sylvia's throat.

"But if I'd just gotten back to our room a little sooner... before it happened."

She fell silent again. Riley knew there was nothing she could say to talk her out of this irrational feeling of guilt.

"I promise you, it wasn't your fault," Riley said. "But it's going to take time to deal with this. You're going to need lots of help."

Sylvia nodded.

Riley said, "Sylvia, can you think of anybody at all who might have meant Drew any harm?"

"No," Sylvia said. "Everybody liked her. You just couldn't help but like her."

Riley said, "Did she happen to mention knowing any of these people—Justin Selves, Joan Cornell, Tony Moore?"

Sylvia shook her head. Riley guessed she had no idea that the other two murders had even happened.

Riley said, "Did she mention ever going to bingo games at Westminster Presbyterian Church?"

"No," Sylvia said.

"You mentioned the chair not being where it was supposed to be," Riley said. "We think it was stolen."

For the first time, Sylvia looked Riley straight in the eye.

"Why?" she said. "It wasn't worth anything."

"Can you tell me where it came from?" Riley asked. "Was it with the apartment when you moved in?"

"Oh, no," Sylvia said. "The apartment was completely unfurnished. Neither one of us had a lot of money, so we bought everything we needed for the place on the cheap—yard sales, garage sales, thrift shops."

Her eyes brightened just a little and she said, "Oh, I remember. We bought it and the other chair and the table at the This-and-That Thrift Store. Drew joked about it at the time. They were matching chairs, and she said they were as nice as the expensive furniture at the store where she'd worked. She said she thought people were dumb to spend so much money there."

Riley felt a tingle of interest.

"Drew worked at a furniture store?" she asked.

"Just over the summer," Sylvia said. "She quit as soon as school started."

"What was the name of the store?" Riley asked.

"Wolfe's Furniture," Sylvia said.

Riley jotted down the name on her notepad. She had a feeling it might be important.

Then she said, "Come on, let's go join your housemates."

Sylvia obediently let Riley help her to her feet. She turned unsteadily and started to walk through the house. Before she followed after her, Riley paused and looked out over the scraggly backyard. A sidewalk cut through the middle of the yard and ended in an alley.

Riley wondered, *Did he leave this way?*

Perhaps he'd parked a car in the alley and planned ahead to use this as an escape route. It certainly would have been easier and less conspicuous than toting a stolen chair out the front door.

But there's no way to know, Riley thought. Plenty of people had been in and out of this house, both the front and back ways, just today.

She turned around and followed Sylvia through the house to the front room. The housemates were all still gathered there. Chief Shore stood watching and listening as Jenn continued asking them questions. Right now they seemed to be in the middle of discussing whether they'd seen anyone unusual around the house lately.

One of the young men remarked, "I saw a guy up on the second floor earlier today. He was a peculiar little guy with a bad haircut and he was carrying some kind of a metal box."

One of the young women told him, "That was Dave, the handyman. He comes around a lot. I'm surprised you haven't noticed him before."

"What was he doing here today?" Jenn asked.

"He was upstairs fixing my kitchen faucet, just like I'd asked him to do," the young woman replied.

"That's right," another housemate said. "Corky and I were home then too. Dave was fixing the faucet."

The one named Corky nodded in agreement.

Riley sighed. That meant that although those three housemates and a repairman had been in the building when the killer struck, they had all been in a second-floor apartment and wouldn't have noticed a stranger in the downstairs hall.

As the housemates discussed other recent comings and goings—friends stopping by to visit somebody who lived here, a deliveryman, boyfriends and girlfriends who'd spend the night, a certain professor who kindly came around with some study materials for a sick student—it became clear that none of those visits had taken place at the time of the murder. It also turned out that, except for the ones with the repairman, the students who lived there hadn't been in the building at all when Drew Cadigan died.

But as the group kept answering Jenn's questions, Riley noticed a palpable tension in the air. Of course everybody felt shaken up that a murder had happened here just a little while ago.

But it's more than that.

Then Riley noticed that the housemates kept glancing over at the front door.

Riley looked herself and realized, *The latch.*

The door latch was still taped so that the door wouldn't lock when somebody closed it. She remembered what Sylvia had said: *"They shouldn't have done that."*

And now at least some of these students were thinking about that latch. Some might be wondering who had taped it like that. Some might know exactly who had done it and harbored deep anger about it.

And at least one of them is feeling as guilty as hell.

And with good reason.

Riley knew it was an issue that was going to hang over this group for at least as long as they kept living here. And whoever was responsible would surely feel guilty for the rest of his or her life.

Would these college kids talk openly about this lapse in communal responsibility, share their feelings of blame and guilt?

For a moment, Riley thought about broaching the subject, just to clear the air. But she quickly decided against it.

I'm not a therapist.

And it had no bearing at all on what she and Jenn were here to do. It was actually none of their business.

Meanwhile, it was clear to Riley that Jenn had asked the housemates all the questions she could. Although none of their answers seemed to have been helpful, it was time for Riley and her colleagues to leave.

It's also late in the day, Riley thought, glancing at her watch.

Riley thanked all the students for their help and encouraged them to seek counseling as soon as possible. Then she, Jenn, and

Chief Shore stepped out onto the front porch, where Riley asked the chief if he knew of any hotels where they could stay the night.

Chief Shore nodded and said that he'd already booked them into the nearby Singer Inn, a small hotel where families often stayed while visiting students at Springett College. He gave them directions on how to get there.

While they were talking, a single TV van pulled up in front of the house.

Riley groaned under her breath.

It's starting.

Because of this third murder, the media had finally figured out that a serial killer might be on the loose. This was just the beginning of what would soon be a media frenzy.

As a cameraman, a sound technician, and a reporter climbed out of the van, Chief Shore said to Riley and Jenn, "I'll handle them. You two get on out of here."

"Thanks," Riley said.

Shore added, "And don't worry, I won't give them any meaningful information. It'll be 'no comment this, no comment that,' and practically nothing else. I know how to handle this."

"That's good," Riley said. "And whatever you do, make sure your cops keep the media away from the kids inside the house."

Chief Shore nodded and walked down to meet the reporter. Meanwhile, Riley and Jenn hurried on to their own borrowed vehicle.

When Riley started the engine and began to drive toward the hotel, Jenn murmured, "I hate this."

Riley didn't reply. She wasn't sure what Jenn meant, but there were certainly plenty of things to hate about the situation right now.

Then Jenn added, "We didn't stop him from killing again."

"I know," Riley said.

Jenn heaved a long, resigned sigh and said, "Well, at least it's over."

Riley glanced at her partner with surprise.

"What do you mean?" she asked.

"Well, obviously, we caught the killer. We caught him too late to save Drew Cadigan, but at least he's not going to kill anybody else."

Riley was startled by how certain Jenn sounded.

She said, "We're not sure Tony Moore's the killer."

"He's guilty, Riley," Jenn said. "We both know it. And tomorrow we can wrap things up and head back to Quantico."

Riley didn't know what to say. She knew Jenn had a tendency to jump to conclusions. On the other hand...

Is she maybe right this time?

As she kept on driving, she replayed the vague feelings she'd gotten of the killer back in the victim's apartment—especially her sense that the killer had seemed pleasant for at least a moment when he'd walked through that door. Then she remembered the booze-sodden punk they'd interviewed in the police station.

Was Tony Moore capable of exercising even the slightest bit of personal charm?

Was he really capable of such a crime?

Riley doubted it very much.

Which means we've still got a lot of work to do.

And they might not have much time before somebody else wound up dead.

CHAPTER THIRTEEN

There was a strange, chilly silence between Riley and Jenn during the rest of the drive to the hotel. Riley could tell that her young partner felt defensive about the question of Tony Moore's guilt or innocence. In fact, Jenn seemed to positively *want* him to be guilty.

Maybe it's understandable, Riley thought.

After all, Riley wanted to solve this case as quickly as possible as much as Jenn did. But she knew that wishful thinking wasn't going to help.

Riley also thought there might be something more to Jenn's strange mood. She had the same uneasy feeling she'd had since they'd met up this morning back in Quantico.

Something was bothering Jenn that she didn't want to talk about.

When they parked in the hotel parking lot and got out of the car, Riley felt on the verge of asking Jenn to open up about what might be wrong. But she remembered the evasive answer she'd already gotten twice today.

"What would be wrong?"

Riley figured there was no point in forcing the issue. She just hoped that whatever was on Jenn's mind didn't start interfering with their work together.

When they checked into the hotel and headed for their separate rooms, they agreed to get together in Riley's room after they'd both showered. Riley ordered a pizza and soft drinks to be delivered to her room so they'd have something to eat while they talked about the case.

As she finished her shower, Riley found herself thinking about what Sylvia had asked her. When she'd told the murdered girl's roommate about her own murdered friends back when she'd been in college, Sylvia had wanted to know, *"How did you cope?"*

Riley sighed as she put on her bathrobe and toweled her hair dry. It was a huge, unanswerable question, and one that would probably trouble Sylvia all her life—and perhaps all of her housemates as well.

Riley was just coming out of the bathroom when there was a knock on the door. It was the pizza deliveryman. Riley paid him and set the pizza and soft drinks down on the table. She was about to call Jenn and tell her supper was ready when her cell phone rang.

The call was from Chief Shore.

He said, "I'm sorry to bother you late like this. But I've got some news I figured you'd want to hear."

Riley's heart quickened as she wondered, *Good news or bad news?*

Chief Shore went on, "When I got back to the station after dealing with the media at the apartment house, I confronted Tony Moore about the new murder. I told him what you'd told me—that his boss said he'd gone missing from work during the time the murder had taken place."

Shore grunted a little.

"Well, naturally, that panicked him some. But he said he had an airtight alibi. He said he'd gotten bored at work and headed out to Kelsey's Place, a bar right across the street from the LangMart store. He said he spent a couple of hours there guzzling Bloody Marys. Not hard to believe, the way his breath smelled when you and Roston brought him in."

Riley remembered that smell vividly. She'd thought it was one good reason to think that Tony wasn't the guy who had charmed his way into Drew Cadigan's room.

"Did you check out his alibi?" she asked.

"I sure did. I called the bar and talked to the bartender. Tony was a regular, and the bartender knew him all too well. Not only was Tony there that whole time, he made a nuisance of himself, harassing the women customers. The bartender finally told him he had to leave. He also remembered the exact time when he kicked Tony out."

Riley's heart sank.

"Don't tell me," she said. "It was shortly before my partner and I found him at the LangMart store."

"Right," Chief Shore said. "Moore obviously headed right back there after he got kicked out of Kelsey's place. There's no way he could have murdered Drew Cadigan while he was between those two locations."

Riley stifled a discouraged sigh.

Chief Shore added, "We'll keep Moore in custody. We've got other stuff to charge him with, including a hit and run. He won't be going free for quite a while. But it looks like we've still got a killer to catch."

"It sure does," Riley said. "We'll have to find another direction. My partner and I will be going over the case tonight. I'll call you first thing tomorrow morning."

Riley ended the call and stared at the phone for a moment. Of course this wasn't unexpected, but even so she felt sharply disappointed. Worse, she knew that the real killer was out there somewhere, probably planning his next murder.

If he hasn't committed it already.

At that moment there came a tap on the adjoining doors between her room and Jenn's. Riley opened the door on her side, and Jenn came on in.

Riley said to her, "I've got bad news. Tony Moore isn't our guy."

Jenn's eyes widened as Riley explained about the phone call she'd just gotten from Chief Shore.

Jenn said, "OK, so we know he didn't kill Drew Cadigan. Does he have alibis for the other two killings?"

Riley was startled by the question.

She said, "Jenn, he didn't kill those people."

"How do you know?" Jenn insisted.

"How can you *not* know?" Riley asked. "Both you and I know that this last killing wasn't the work of a copycat. Nobody even had enough information to duplicate the murders."

"Maybe he's got an accomplice," Jenn said. "If so, all we've got to do is get him to tell us—"

Riley interrupted sharply, "He doesn't have an accomplice. It's our job to profile these killers. And while we don't know much about this one, I'm sure he acts alone, and you should be sure of it too. We've studied these things, we've got experience. We know he's not the type to share whatever kind of gratification he's getting out of these killings."

Jenn didn't reply. She stared off into space for a moment, then sat down at the table.

Something's really wrong about her, Riley decided.

And she figured it was time to clear the air about whatever it was.

But before Riley could start asking questions, her phone buzzed again. This time the call was from home.

She picked up the phone and heard Jilly's frantic voice, "Mom, we've got a big problem. It's April."

Riley felt panic rising.

"Has something happened to your sister?" she asked.

"Not exactly, but it's really bad," Jilly said. "April thinks she can just come and go whenever and wherever she wants."

Riley knitted her brow.

"I—I'm not sure I understand," she said.

"Well, April's grounded, isn't she? I mean, she fired a gun in the house. She could have killed somebody. That's really, really bad. So you told her she was grounded, right? She can't just go running around all over the place, right?"

Riley felt thoroughly baffled now.

Did I tell April she was grounded?

She really couldn't remember.

She asked Jilly, "Is your sister out of the house right now?"

"No, she's down in the family room, but—"

Riley interrupted, "Go tell her I want to talk to her."

"OK," Jilly said. "Be sure to tell her she's grounded."

Riley heard the clatter of Jilly setting down the phone, then her footsteps walking away.

Meanwhile, Riley saw that Jenn was still sitting at the table looking blankly at the pizza.

Riley said, "Uh, Jenn, I've got something I need to handle with the kids. In private, if you don't mind."

Jenn got up from her chair and said, "Some kind of a sisters problem?"

"Yeah, I guess you could say that," Riley said. "I'm sorry, this might take a while. Take some pizza with you. Eat it before it gets cold. And take something to drink too."

Jenn scooped up three slices of pizza into napkins and picked up a canned soft drink. She walked to the door, then turned to Riley and said, "Tell your kids they should be nice to each other. They're lucky to have each other. Siblings are … well, there's nothing as important as a brother or sister."

Jenn had an odd look in her eye. Riley wondered what she meant.

But before she could ask, Jenn opened the door to her own room and added, "I'll see you tomorrow."

She left, closing the door behind her.

Then Riley heard April's voice over the phone.

"Mom, Jilly's acting all crazy. She says I'm grounded. You never said I was grounded. I'm not grounded, am I?"

Riley struggled to remember just what she had told April after the gun incident.

I ought to have grounded her, she thought.

But did I?

She said to April, "Where is it you want to go?"

"To soccer practice, that's all," April said. "The team's got practice tomorrow after school. We've got a big game over the weekend, so it's really important that I go to all the practices this week. I can go, can't I?"

Riley was startled by how overwhelmed she suddenly felt. Even after a day of investigating murders, this seemed like an insurmountable problem.

But I've got to make a decision.

She thought for a moment, then said, "Soccer practice is a responsibility. Of course you can go."

"So I'm not grounded?" April asked.

"I didn't say that."

"So what *are* you saying? You've already decided I don't get to have a gun anymore. Isn't that enough of a punishment?"

Riley was pacing the room now.

Trying to sound more self-assured than she felt, she said, "April, you know perfectly well that what you did was very serious. We should have talked more about the consequences. I don't want you to go anywhere else until I get back and we can talk things over."

"Not even to the mall?" April said in a pleading voice.

"Definitely not to the mall," Riley said.

April whined, "Mo-o-o-m!"

Her patience slipping, Riley snapped, "I need for you to act grown up, April. I'm dealing with three murdered people here in the Philly suburbs, and I'm trying to stop whoever did it from killing anyone else, and for all I know I'm already too late. So don't argue with me, please. I can't handle it right now."

Sounding startled, April said, "OK. I'm sorry."

"Now go tell your sister we've worked everything out. And that you can go to soccer practice."

"OK."

They ended the call, then Riley immediately remembered what Jenn had said to her just now.

"Tell your kids they should be nice to each other."

And also ...

"There's nothing as important as a brother or sister."

Riley hadn't gotten around to saying those things to April or Jilly. She wondered—should she call the girls back and share Jenn's message? She quickly decided against it. She felt like she might lose her temper if she had to talk to either of the girls right now.

It can wait until I get back home.

But as Riley sat down to eat her pizza, she found herself wondering, *What did Jenn mean by that, anyway?*

Why was Jenn so concerned about how April and Jilly were getting along? It wasn't like Jenn to take much interest in Riley's family life. She wondered if maybe she should go over to Jenn's room next door and ask her about it.

But again, Riley worried about how thin her patience had become. She and Jenn seemed to be mysteriously at odds, and if they tried to work things out right now, they might end up arguing. That was the last thing either of them needed right now.

Riley took a few more bites of pizza but quickly realized she'd lost her appetite. More than that, she was deeply tired after a long and discouraging day. She decided she and Jenn would go over the details of the case first thing in the morning. They'd figure out what to investigate next, and they'd get back to work on it.

She brushed her teeth and climbed into bed.

As she started to drift off to sleep, anxieties and worries drifted through her mind.

She wasn't happy with how she'd dealt with the girls over the phone. But then, she hadn't handled things very well when she'd still been at home. She should have laid down stricter rules for April to follow after the gun incident. If she had, the girls wouldn't have quarreled about it, and there wouldn't even have been a phone call, no sudden family crisis for Riley to deal with.

It was my fault, Riley thought miserably.

She also felt troubled by the unnecessary force she'd used against Tony Moore.

Again she realized, *I'm bringing my home life into my work.*

Her anxieties seemed to multiply as she drifted off to sleep. She was grateful for sleep, but with all the turmoil in her head, she felt sure she was going to have nightmares.

CHAPTER FOURTEEN

Riley found herself wandering inside a building that reminded her of the LangMart store, except that it was even more vast and labyrinthine. As she looked down one aisle, it disappeared into a vanishing point in the far distance. She guessed that the store went on for untold miles in all directions. She couldn't imagine just how far.

She quickly saw that this wasn't a hypermarket that sold the usual range of consumer goods. Instead, it appeared to be some kind of home furnishing store, with mocked up rooms everywhere exhibiting furniture, fixtures, rugs, and types of flooring.

But what am I doing here?

And how did I get here?

There was no one to ask—not another customer in sight, and no service people either.

The light was very dim. She felt almost as though she'd fallen asleep in the store and awakened after hours to find herself completely alone here...

Or maybe not so alone.

She heard voices coming from somewhere—cheerful, laughing voices.

She followed the voices until she came to a mock-up dining room, the only display she'd seen so far that was fully lit. The ghostly voices seemed to be coming from right here—although they were strangely garbled and impossible to understand.

As Riley's eyes adjusted to the brighter light, the room struck her as strangely out of place in this store. The style of decor and furnishings seemed out of date. But more than that, the room didn't look like the other pristine and spotless displays surrounding her.

It was tidy and clean, but also a little frayed and worn in places...

As if someone actually lived here.

Then she felt a jolt of shock as she saw that there were actual people seated at the dining room table…

Dead people!

She recognized their faces—and also their slashed throats.

At one end of the table sat the corpse of Justin Selves, slouching awkwardly in the chair with his eyes closed. At the other end of the table, slumping in a similar manner and also with closed eyes, was Joan Cornell's body. Seated on far side of the table was Drew Cadigan's corpse, her eyes wide open and her wound looking fresher than the others.

As Riley looked more closely, she noticed something odd about the chairs where the corpses were seated. It took her a moment to realize—she'd seen those same styles of chairs at the two crime scenes she'd visited, and also in the police photos taken of Justin Selves's murder.

She suddenly knew what they were.

The stolen chairs!

Here they were, and the corpses of the people who had owned them were seated in them.

Meanwhile, the happy but incomprehensible chatter continued, sounding as if the corpses were talking together…

Like at a family dinner.

Meanwhile, the table itself seemed to be constantly changing in shape and length, and the number of empty chairs at the table kept changing as well.

Riley wondered, What does it mean?

She shuddered with horror as she thought of one way to find out.

I'll join them for dinner.

Then I'll ask them.

Shaking from head to foot, her heart pounding with fear, Riley forced herself to take a step toward one of the empty chairs, then another, then another…

Riley's eyes snapped open, and she found herself sweating and gasping in her hotel room bed. Morning light was peeking between the window curtains.

It was a dream, she thought with relief.

She realized now that she'd been having nightmares all during the night. But she remembered the last one most vividly—the dream of the corpses seated in purloined chairs as if at a family meal.

In the dream, she had been about to join them.

Riley sat up and rubbed her eyes.

She knew better than to ignore dreams as shocking, intense, and real as this. Sometimes those dreams gave her intuitive insights that she didn't always get when she was awake. And so far during this case, her gut instincts hadn't felt especially sharp.

This might be just what I need, she thought.

She replayed the dream in her head, remembering the garbled chatter, the propped up corpses, the stolen chairs.

She also remembered the questions that had troubled her at the scene of Drew Cadigan's murder. Of all the murderers Riley had ever hunted down who had taken souvenirs, this one was strange and unique.

The other souvenir-takers had usually been driven by a desire to revisit and relive the sexual gratification of their murders.

But what's sexual about a chair?

Nothing that she could think of, and yet... *It feels like an intimate gesture.*

It also felt strangely and inexplicably sad.

As she struggled to put her thoughts together, she felt as though she could again hear all that cheerful, disembodied chatter.

Like a family.

It began to dawn on Riley that the very concept of *family* was central to the killer's actions.

But in what way?

And wasn't it possible that Riley was misinterpreting her own dream? She'd been fretting about family problems when she'd gone to sleep. Wouldn't it be natural for her to have a dream that hinted at family life? Maybe the murders had nothing to do with family at all.

Riley quickly decided she should brainstorm with Jenn about her nightmare while it was still fresh in her mind. Riley threw on a robe and knocked on the doors between her room and Jenn's. No one answered. Riley opened the door on her side, then noticed that Jenn's door was slightly ajar.

Jenn must be up already, Riley thought.

Riley pushed the door open and called out Jenn's name. No reply came. The bathroom door was standing open, so Jenn obviously wasn't taking a morning shower.

Maybe she'd already gone to breakfast without her. If so, Riley wasn't going to be very happy about that.

Then as she looked around, she wondered, *Where are Jenn's things?*

She didn't see Jenn's go-bag anywhere, and the open closet was empty of any clothing. The bed was still made as if nobody had slept there, so there was no sign that anybody was even staying in this room.

Riley felt her pulse quicken as she sensed that something was very wrong.

She glanced around the room again.

A folded piece of hotel stationery was on the nightstand beside the bed.

Riley walked over to the nightstand, picked up the paper, and read it.

Riley,
I'm sorry.
Jenn

Riley let out gasp of shock and confusion.

Jenn was gone.

But where had she gone?

And why?

CHAPTER FIFTEEN

For a moment, Riley wondered if she might be having another anxiety-fueled dream...

Maybe this isn't happening.

But she knew it was no dream. The deserted hotel room was all too real.

The only sign that her partner had ever been here was the note Riley was now holding in her hand, with its mysterious two-word message...

I'm sorry.

Riley wondered—sorry for what? And where had Jenn gone, anyway?

She felt a flicker of anger.

I should have expected something like this, she thought.

She'd known all day yesterday that something wasn't right with Jenn. But she hadn't pushed the issue. And now Riley was starting to feel angry with herself as well as with Jenn...

I should have insisted that she tell me.

But maybe it wasn't too late for explanations.

Riley returned to her own room and picked up her cell phone. She dialed Jenn's number. She heard Jenn's recorded voice blandly reciting her familiar outgoing message. At the sound of the beep, Riley said in a voice that shook with anger and frustration...

"Jenn, what the hell's going on? Where are you? And what's this note supposed to mean? Call me *right away*. And you'd better have a pretty damn good explanation. More than that, you'd better get your ass back here. Now!"

The phone trembled in Riley's hand as she ended the call.

She sat down on the bed and told herself...

She'll call back.

She'll call me any minute.

But Riley couldn't help but doubt it. And now what was she supposed to do? The proper procedure, of course, was to call Brent Meredith right away to alert him that her partner had gone AWOL.

But I can't do that.

Her relationship with Jenn was much too interwoven and complicated for that. They'd only known each other since last spring, but it seemed to Riley like much longer. They'd been through a lot together during that short time, solving several cases and sharing dangers and risks and even saving each other's lives.

Riley knew from experience that those kinds of experiences formed strong bonds of friendship and loyalty. And Riley and Jenn had been plenty loyal to each other, sometimes bending and even breaking BAU rules along the way.

Riley especially remembered the first time they had worked together, back in April. Bill had been on mandatory leave because of PTSD after a shootout that had gone bad. Jenn had been assigned as Riley's partner. In the middle of their work on a case in Iowa, Riley had received a terrifying phone text from Bill...

"Been sitting here with a gun in my mouth."

Riley had gone AWOL herself that time, flying straight back to Virginia to help Bill. Jenn had kept working on the case on her own, covering for Riley's absence without asking any questions. Riley and Bill had done the same for Jenn in May, when she had briefly vanished while the three of them were working on another case together.

Riley still didn't know any details about why Jenn had disappeared that time, but she did know...

It had something to do with Aunt Cora.

Riley shuddered at the thought...

Maybe it's happening again.

Of course, when Riley had asked Jenn yesterday whether Aunt Cora had been in touch with her, Jenn had said "no" flat-out.

But had Jenn been lying?

Maybe Aunt Cora was again exerting her insidious influence over Jenn, trying to draw her back into her criminal web.

If so, Riley wondered...

Will she ever come back?

It dawned on Riley that she might have one way of finding out. But it wasn't an option she liked.

Aunt Cora had once called Riley by phone, offering a valuable but unsolicited tip on a murder case. It had been an unsettling experience, and Riley had wondered ever since whether she might someday pay dearly for the information Aunt Cora had given her.

And now...

Maybe the bill has come due.

Riley's hands felt cold as she fingered her cell phone. The number Aunt Cora had used to call her was still stored in its caller list. As much as she dreaded the idea, Riley had to at least try to get in touch with the sinister criminal mastermind.

She found the number and put through the call. But she immediately heard a message saying that the number was no longer in service.

Riley let out a discouraged sigh.

It was no surprise, of course. She knew Aunt Cora was much too shrewd at covering her tracks to leave behind a working phone number, especially after all this time.

Riley decided she had no real choice right now.

She would have to keep on working without her partner, hoping against hope that Jenn would soon come back. And she wasn't going to call Meredith about it, either. She hated to be dishonest with a boss whom she admired and respected, but it wouldn't be the first time.

Rules be damned, she thought.

Riley got dressed and went downstairs to join other hotel guests for a light breakfast. She sat down at a table alone with a cup of coffee and a Danish, then checked her watch.

It was time for her to touch base with Chief Shore.

She punched the chief's number into her cell phone.

"Good morning, Agent Paige," Shore said. "Have you got any fresh ideas?"

"I'm mulling something over," Riley said. "How about you?"

Shore grunted slightly and said, "Well, it looks like I've got a busy morning ahead. I'm still dealing with the media, of course, and I'm making a statement in front of cameras in a little while."

"Anything you need me for?" Riley said.

"No, it might even be best not to have you there. I'm planning to tell them as little as possible. All there is to say, really, is that we've had three killings, and we don't yet have any viable suspects, and that the grisly details are none of their damn business. I can do that by myself. There's no reason to put yourself in their sights at this point. The less you have to deal with them, the better."

Riley silently agreed. She was glad the chief looked at things that way. Lots of times, local authorities were all too eager to show off the fact that they had FBI muscle at their disposal. Sometimes they even did that so the FBI would take the blame for any mistakes.

Chief Shore added, "After that I've got an appointment with the coroner about his autopsy on Drew Cadigan. Pretty much a formality, of course. We all have a pretty good idea how she died."

Yes, we certainly do, Riley thought.

Chief Shore said, "Sometime today I want to go back to yesterday's murder scene, take another look at things. What about you? What have you got planned?"

Riley thought for a second, then said, "I'm working on an idea. I'll let you know how it pans out."

"Be sure to do that," Chief Shore said.

As they ended the call, Riley felt relieved that Shore didn't expect to meet with her and Jenn this morning. She didn't want to try to explain why her partner wasn't with her. She'd felt awkward enough using the first person singular during their conversation—*I* and not *we*. She was glad he hadn't asked her about that.

Meanwhile, a germ of an idea was forming in her head.

She took a sip of coffee and remembered again last night's nightmare, and those three corpses sitting at a dining room table...

With plenty of room for company.

And now, she had a deepening hunch that the murders had something to do with *family*. She didn't yet understand just how or why, but she thought she might know where to start trying to find out.

Sylvia had told Riley yesterday that Drew had worked over the summer at a furniture store. That had struck Riley as an interesting detail in a murder case that involved stolen furniture. Trying to think of the store's name, Riley took out her notes from her interview with Sylvia and found it.

Wolfe's Furniture.

In her notes Riley also found the name of the store where Sylvia and Drew had bought their own kitchen furniture—the This-and-That Thrift Store. Riley felt sure that neither of the other two victims had bought their furniture at a thrift store. They were much too well off, and their furniture had been of better quality.

Judging from what Sylvia had told her, Wolfe's Furniture was definitely a higher-end store—the kind of place where both of the other victims may have shopped.

She decided that it was time for her to find out more about furniture.

Riley used her cell phone to find the store's address and directions on how to get there. Then she finished her coffee and Danish and headed out to the borrowed vehicle.

It felt weird to be starting out the day alone like this.

More than that, Jenn's disappearance truly worried her.

Put it out of your head, Riley thought as she started driving.

You've got a case to solve.

CHAPTER SIXTEEN

When Riley walked inside Wolfe's Furniture, the place eerily reminded her of last night's dream. It was an expansive store filled with all kinds of room displays, with furniture that somehow struck her as both expensive looking and blandly uninteresting.

But unlike in her dream, the displays here weren't fully mocked up individual rooms separated by walls. Riley could see all the way to across the show room, which didn't disappear into a seemingly infinite distance. And the lighting everywhere was almost painfully bright.

Riley heard a woman ask in a musical-sounding voice ...

"How may I help you?"

Riley turned and was startled by the smiling face she saw.

Where have I seen that face?

Then came a shock of recognition. The young employee's face looked uncannily like that of Drew Cadigan's corpse. She had the same rusty red hair and porcelain skin. But most of all ...

The eyes.

Just like the dead woman who had stared vacantly up from the apartment floor, this young woman's eyes were a vibrant blue. She wore a nameplate that said TARA. The resemblance seemed so uncanny that Riley simply had to wonder—was Tara related to Drew Cadigan? Perhaps even her sister?

For a moment, Riley didn't know what to say. Then she reminded herself of why she'd come here.

She said, "I would like to speak to the manager if that's possible."

"May I ask what this is about?" Tara asked.

Tara's eyes widened as Riley pulled out her badge and introduced herself.

"I'd just like to ask the manager a few questions," she said.

"Of course," Tara said. "I'll go get him."

Tara wandered away toward a door marked OFFICE. Riley turned and glanced around the store, only to be startled anew by the face of the young woman sitting at a table with a furniture catalogue and a calculator.

She too had red hair, and although her complexion was ruddier than either Drew's or Tara's, there still seemed to be a resemblance among them. She had a name plate that said SERENA, and she was looking at Riley with an expression of intense interest.

Riley felt even more nonplussed that before. She now wondered whether both of these women were closely related to Drew Cadigan. If so, did they have any idea what had happened to Drew just yesterday?

Just then a tall man came striding out of the office toward Riley. He was a startlingly aristocratic-looking gentleman of about Riley's age, and he was wearing an extremely elegant three-piece suit with a silk scarf in place of a tie. The corner of a precisely folded white silk handkerchief poked out of his jacket pocket.

Walking toward Riley, he said in a purring tone…

"FBI, are we? I'm afraid I don't like the sound of that. Come, sit down."

He led Riley toward the table where the young woman named Serena was sitting. Without being told, Serena got up from the table and walked away. Riley and the man sat facing each other at the table.

He said, "My name is Cassius Wolfe, and I own the store. It's been in my family for three generations, I'm proud to say. Now kindly tell me exactly who you are and what brings you here."

Although he didn't exactly have an English accent, he spoke in what seemed to Riley like carefully enunciated upper-class English cadences. She felt sure he'd gone to a lot of trouble to cultivate that way of talking.

Riley took out her badge and introduced herself again.

Then she said, "I understand you had an employee working here this summer named Drew Cardigan."

Leaning back in his chair, Wolfe said, "Oh, dear. Has Drew done something illegal? I hate to say it, but I wouldn't be surprised."

Slightly startled, Riley asked, "Why do you say that?"

"Well, she had something of an attitude problem when she was working here."

"How so?" Riley asked.

"To put it charitably to her, she and I didn't exactly see eye to eye. She was also not an especially honest girl, as I found out in a rather disagreeable way. She came to work here last June, gave me the strong impression that she wanted long-term employment. Instead she quit on me quite abruptly. She had to go back to school, she said. It was the first time she'd mentioned school of any sort."

Riley could understand the man's resentment, even if she didn't sympathize. Drew Cadigan was hardly the first young woman to take a summer job without mentioning she'd be a short-timer. Riley herself had done that a couple of times during her youth. She'd felt a little guilty for misleading her employers, but it had been the only way to get those jobs.

She said, "I'm sorry to say that she was murdered yesterday."

Wolfe's eyes widened.

"My god," he said. "I had no idea. This is terrible."

Riley said, "We're afraid that this is the work of a serial killer, and that there are more killings to come. There have been two other victims—Justin Selves and Joan Cornell. Did you know either of those people?"

"Not that I can remember," Wolfe said.

Riley's eyes narrowed as she asked, "I'd like to look through your sales records to find out if either or both of them made purchases here."

Wolfe chuckled slightly, "Well, I'm afraid I can't allow that."

"Why not?" Riley said.

Wolfe tilted his head back and said, "I like to think I have a rather special relationship with my clients. And yes, I *do* think of them as clients rather than mere customers. What if word got out that I was allowing the FBI to poke through my records looking for information on them?"

Riley was truly surprised now.

She said, "Mr. Wolfe, these two *clients* happen to be *dead.*"

"Nevertheless," Wolfe said. "It's a matter of principle, as I expect you to understand. Of course, if it matters as much as you seem to think it does, I suppose you could get a warrant."

Riley suppressed a growl of annoyance.

She supposed she *could* get a warrant. But she hadn't imagined in coming here that she might need one. She didn't want to waste time with that, but she didn't want to waste time arguing with this annoying man either.

"Of course," she said to Wolfe. "I'll probably do that."

"Will there be anything else?" Wolfe asked.

Riley studied his haughty expression for a moment. Then she turned and looked at the two young women who worked for him. They were huddled closely together some distance away, whispering to each other and eyeing Riley with furtive expressions.

Riley looked back at Wolfe and said, "I can't help wonder—are the young women who work for you related somehow?"

Wolfe's eyes narrowed.

"Why do you ask?"

Riley shrugged slightly and said, "Well, there's such a strong resemblance—not just between these two, but also the victim, and—"

Wolfe interrupted sharply, "Agent Paige, I'm sure that's none of your business. In fact, I can't imagine why you'd ask such a question."

Riley was taken aback by his indignant tone.

Did I touch a nerve? she wondered.

The bell at the front door rang, and Riley could hear the voices of entering customers. Wolfe took the opportunity to rise from his seat.

He said, "And now, if you don't mind, I've got clients to serve."

He walked toward the couple that had just entered. The young woman named Tara was already welcoming them, while the one named Serena was walking toward where Riley was sitting.

Riley wondered—Why was Wolfe so brusquely defensive over what seemed to her like a fairly innocuous question?

What on earth is going on here?

She just started to get up from her chair when Serena plopped a folded piece of paper on the table right in front of her. Written on the paper were these words...

Don't read until after you leave.

Riley glanced over at Serena, who now seemed to be trying to appear completely uninterested in Riley's presence. Riley pocketed the note, went outside, and got into her car.

She unfolded the note, which said...

Come back in 15 minutes. Mr. Wolfe will be gone. We can talk.

Riley's eyes widened with surprise.

Was she about to find out much more than she'd expected?

CHAPTER SEVENTEEN

R iley read the note over two or three times, trying to decide what to make of it. She'd gotten a very bad feeling about Cassius Wolfe, and now these women wanted to talk to her after he left.

What do they want to tell me? she wondered. *Something about him? Or just something they don't want him to know they're talking about?*

Either way, Riley felt more than willing to comply.

Meanwhile, she knew she ought to make herself as inconspicuous as possible. She pulled the car out of the parking lot, then drove it around the block until she found an open parking space on the street where she could see the store.

It felt strange to be sitting alone in a car while she was working. She was used to having a partner—someone to share ideas with, or just to engage in irrelevant conversation to pass time and relieve tension.

Again she wondered…

Where is Jenn?

Part of Riley felt that she should be trying find the answer to that question right this minute. But that wasn't possible. She had a job to do, with or without Jenn's aid.

Riley sat waiting for the full fifteen minutes. During that time, she saw the couple that had arrived to shop for furniture come back outside and drive away in their car. Finally, right on schedule, Cassius Wolfe emerged from his store and began to walk down the street away from her. Riley felt sure he hadn't noticed her.

As soon as Wolfe was out of sight, Riley got out of the car and returned to the store. When she walked inside the two young women hurried over to meet her.

They both had troubled expressions on their young faces.

Tara said, "Thank you for coming back, Agent Paige."

Serena said, "This is Mr. Wolfe's break time. He always goes down the street to his favorite café. He'll be gone for half an hour, pretty much exactly. That will give us time to talk."

"Talk about what?" Riley asked.

Serena and Tara glanced at each other.

Then Serena said to Riley, "I overheard you saying something about Drew. Did something happen to her?"

Riley nodded and said, "I'm sorry to have to tell you—Drew is dead. Yesterday she was the victim of a murder."

Serena's mouth dropped open.

"Oh, no," she said. "That's terrible."

Riley asked, "Did the two of you know her very well?"

"I did," Serena whispered. "Fairly well, anyhow. We worked together over the summer. I've been working here for a whole year now."

"I never met her," Tara said. "I got hired recently to replace her when she left."

"Horrible," Serena muttered, her eyes filling with tears. "How could such a thing happen?"

"The FBI is looking into it," Riley told her. "That's why I'm here."

"Do you think that Mr. Wolfe..." Tara began.

"He's not currently a suspect," Riley said. "Gathering information from everyone who knew the victim is standard procedure."

The two women were staring back at her wide-eyed, as though they both wanted to say something more.

"Of course we also need to know the whereabouts of anyone who might come under suspicion," Riley added. "Drew was murdered at about four o'clock yesterday afternoon. Do you know where Mr. Wolfe was at the time?"

Serena and Tara glanced at each other.

"He was right here," Serena said.

"Are you sure?" Riley asked.

"Oh, yes," Tara said. "He was here the whole afternoon and stayed until we closed."

Riley felt a twinge of disappointment, but she wasn't really surprised. As despicable as Wolfe seemed to be, she hadn't gotten the impression that he was capable of murder.

As she looked at the two young women, Riley felt a new flash of puzzlement at their resemblance to each other and to Drew. She'd already wondered if they were all related. But if one of them didn't even know Drew, that didn't seem likely.

She remembered Wolfe's sharp reply when she'd asked about that resemblance…

"Agent Paige, I'm sure that's none of your business."

Why had he reacted that way?

Stammering for the right words, Riley said, "I'm curious… there's such a strong resemblance… I mean, the three of you…"

Serena rolled her eyes and said, "Oh, you mean the red hair. Yeah, we do look a lot alike, don't we? Well, it's because Mr. Wolfe has a *type*."

"A type?" Riley asked.

"A type of girl that he likes to have around," Serena said. "He only hires redheads. And he only hires women—*girls* he always calls us. He hires girls that he considers to be good-looking."

"And single," Tara added.

Serena said, "I can't tell you how many job interviews he did before he hired Tara here—or before me and Drew. He just won't hire anybody until he finds a pretty redhead. The girls who worked here before me told me he's always been that way."

Now Riley understood Wolfe's defensiveness about the issue.

She also felt a wave of disgust.

Wolfe might not be a killer but he certainly saw women as objects. How far did he push them?

Riley said, "While I was talking to Mr. Wolfe just now, he gave me the distinct impression that he and Drew didn't get along."

Serena scoffed. "Oh, that's putting it mildly. Drew never put up with his shenanigans."

"Shenanigans?" Riley asked.

"He's a really creepy man," Serena said. "He's got no sense of personal space, if you know what I mean. He's always standing too close. And he can't keep his hands to himself."

"But that's not even the worst of it," Tara added. "It's the things he says. Like, 'We just got this mattress in. Perhaps you'd like to try it out with me. Wouldn't that be delightful?' Or, 'I'll bet you'd look really nice in a more revealing outfit. Maybe we could go out shopping together.'"

"But he got really bad with Drew," Serena said. "For some reason, he found her especially attractive. He was constantly pestering her to stay after hours or go on dates with him or even come over to his house."

Riley asked, "How did she deal with it?"

Serena said, "Well, she didn't put up with it. She didn't feel like she had to. This was only a summer job as far as she was concerned, although Mr. Wolfe didn't know that at the time, so she wasn't afraid of getting fired. When she *did* finally quit, he really went through the roof."

Riley's brain clicked away as she tried to make sense of what she was hearing.

She said, "Why do his other female employees put up with it?"

"Like Tara and me, you mean?" Serena said. "Well, these aren't summer jobs for us. We need the stability. So we've always just sort of smiled and acted like good sports about the stuff he does."

"But what he's doing is sexual harassment, pure and simple," Riley said. "You should report it."

Serena let out a bitter sigh.

She said, "Agent Paige, I don't think you know the kind of reputation Mr. Wolfe has here in Springett, or how important he is. He's from an old family and everybody around here respects and trusts him."

Riley had the feeling these women had reached some kind of breaking point and had finally had enough of the man's ugly behavior. They didn't want to put up with it anymore.

That's why they wanted to talk to me, she thought. *The man is harassing them.*

The women stood looking at Riley expectantly, as if they expected her to do something.

Riley sternly reminded herself why she was here. She said carefully, "I'd like to help you with your situation. But really, this isn't an FBI matter."

Serena took a long, slow breath and said, "We understand. But things have changed—just this morning."

"Maybe you could just give us some advice," Tara added.

"About what?" Riley asked.

"Come with us," Serena said.

Whatever the matter was, Riley could tell that the women were shaken up about it. She followed them through the store into the employee restroom. It was spacious and clean with expensive-looking fixtures and elegant and fancy wallpaper.

Serena pointed to a spot on the wall and said ...

"Tara noticed this just this morning."

Riley looked closely and saw a tiny round hole bored into the wall. The hole was well camouflaged by a dark pattern in the wallpaper. When she used her cell phone as a light to look inside, she saw a glint of reflection.

A lens, she realized.

Almost with a gasp, she asked the women, "What's on the other side of this wall?"

"His office," Serena said.

Riley turned toward the two women and said, "You know what this is, don't you? It's a peephole."

Tara and Serena both nodded.

"How long has it been here?" Riley asked.

Serena said, "We've got no idea. Maybe it's new. Or maybe it's been here since before I even started working here. Years, maybe. Who knows?"

Tara added, "Like we said, we noticed it just this morning. We weren't sure what to do about it. When we found out you were from the FBI, we thought maybe you could tell us."

Riley felt her face flush with anger.

"You've got to report this," she said. "I don't care how important Mr. Wolfe is, or what everybody in Springett thinks of him. This kind of surveillance is illegal."

"How do we do that?" Serena asked.

Riley thought for a moment, then said …

"Take photographs of this peephole. Contact Chief Shore at the local police department and show the photos to him. I'm sure he'll bring charges against Mr. Wolfe. It's an open-and-shut case. I'll let the chief know about this myself, but *you've* got to be the ones who report it. Do you understand?"

Tara and Serena were staring at Riley now. Riley sensed that they were wavering.

She said, "I know it's scary to do this. But you've got to be strong. You've got to stand up to this perverted bastard. Judging from what you've told me, he's been getting away with despicable behavior for way too long, and he'll keep right on doing it if you don't do something right now. It's time for it to stop."

Both women nodded.

"Thanks so much," Tara said. "We'll do exactly what you say."

"But what about you?" Serena asked. "Did you find out whatever you came here to find out?"

Riley shook her head.

"I'm afraid not," she said. "Before Drew was killed, there were two other victims. We think we're dealing with a serial killer. I was hoping to find out whether either of the other two victims bought furniture here. But Mr. Wolfe won't let me look at the store's records."

Tara and Serena looked at each other, then back at Riley.

"We'll show them to you," Serena said.

Tara nodded in agreement.

Riley was taken aback. She hadn't intended to ask the women for this kind of help. And she certainly hadn't expected them to offer it unasked.

What should I do? she wondered.

It would certainly be bending the rules for the employees to look through those records on Riley's behalf. More than that, Riley might actually be breaking the law...

Or maybe not.

Would it matter that Serena and Tara were offering Riley this information of their own accord?

Riley fought down a growl of impatience. It wasn't like she had time to ask a lawyer about this right now. Even waiting for a search warrant might take too long. For all she knew, the killer had taken another victim already.

She nodded and said, "OK, let's do it."

She followed the women out of the restroom and back to the sales table, where Serena sat down at the store's computer. Riley told Serena the names she was looking for.

Serena's fingers clicked away at the keyboard for a few seconds.

"Yes, here they are," she said. "Justin Selves and his wife bought a new dining room set a month ago. And Joan Cornell came here on the same day and bought a dining room set of her own."

Riley's curiosity was piqued.

"Can you tell me who made the sale?" she asked Serena.

"Yes," Serena said. "Drew handled it."

Riley felt a tingle of excitement. She realized what this might mean. The killer might have been right here that very day and chosen all three of his potential victims on the spot. She thought hard and fast to consider all the possibilities.

She asked Serena, "Were you working here that day?"

"No, I don't think so," Serena said.

Riley's brow wrinkled in thought. Serena wouldn't be able to identify anyone suspicious who might have been here at the time. Still, Riley could think of other possible suspects.

Riley asked, "What about movers? You must have people who work for you regularly."

Serena nodded.

"The Brennan Brothers do all our moving," she said. "They're really good guys. I'm sure they wouldn't hurt a fly."

Riley knew there was no point in trying to explain to Serena that some of the most brutal killers managed to seem like kindly, gentle people.

Instead she asked, "Did the Brennan Brothers move the furniture for those people that day?"

"I'm sure they did," Serena said, adding, "And they always send the same three people—Nick and Greg Brennan and their hired man, Carlos."

Riley took out her computer pad and brought up information about the first two murders—the exact times and dates when they had happened. Serena quickly checked and found that the Brennan Brothers had been busy moving merchandise for Wolfe Furniture at those very times.

They've got alibis too, Riley realized.

Riley took another look around the store and saw a couple of well-positioned security cameras. Perhaps they'd caught an image of the killer when he was in the very act of choosing his victims.

She asked Serena, "Could I get a look at the store's security tapes?"

Serena shook her head and said, "I'm afraid not. We'd have go get into Mr. Wolfe's office, and even then, only he has got access to them. And besides, I'm not sure he keeps footage that far back."

Riley fought down a groan of discouragement.

She wasn't sure what she was going to do with the information she'd just gotten, but she knew her choices weren't going to be easy.

Riley thanked Tara and Serena for their valuable help and sternly reminded them that they simply *had* to report Cassius

Wolfe's behavior, especially the peephole. Then she left the store and headed back to her car.

As soon as she sat behind the wheel, she saw Cassius Wolfe returning from his coffee break. She breathed a sigh of relief as she realized she'd gotten out of the store just in the nick of time.

Watching Wolfe's smug stride as he walked toward his store, Riley smiled a little.

He's got no idea what he's in for.

She had no doubt that he'd soon be up to his neck in a well-deserved harassment case, with perhaps a whole army of former female employees coming back to haunt him.

At least one good thing came from this visit, she thought.

She also felt pretty sure that she'd found both the time and place where the killer had begun to stalk his victims.

But she needed to know much, much more.

And how was she going to find it out?

She sat in the car considering her next course of action. She wondered about the possible existence of security tapes from that day. Even if they still existed, she knew there was no guarantee that they caught any images of the killer. He might not have even gone inside the store to choose his victims.

Still, it was probably worth trying to get a subpoena for them.

I'll have to talk with Chief Shore about that.

Meanwhile, she'd just learned something about the killer that she hadn't known before. And she had a pretty good idea of how and where she might put that knowledge to use.

I'll drive there right now, she thought.

But first she had a phone call to make.

She took out her cell phone and started to punch in a number.

Chapter Eighteen

The man stood gazing at the dining room table, fairly happy with what he'd accomplished so far.

But I'm not finished yet, he reminded himself.

Far from it.

It was a nice enough table, just the right size, and close enough to the one he'd sat at in his youth.

Right now there were four chairs placed exactly where they ought to be.

There was a chair for Mom at one end, and another for Dad at the other end.

A chair for his sister Maureen was placed to Mom's left alongside the table, and another for himself was right next to Maureen's, closer to Dad.

Three framed pictures were placed on the table in front of Mom, Dad, and Mo.

The room was lit only by candles, and as he peered closely at the chairs he wondered about the people who should be in them...

Are they here?

If they were, could he see them yet?

Yes, he could just begin to detect their shadowy forms seated in their proper places—Mom so willowy and elegant, Dad so strong and vigorous, and Maureen looking so grown up and pretty.

He wasn't seated with them, of course.

He wanted to join them, but he couldn't do that until two more chairs were in place, facing across the table from his and Mo's.

He asked the shadows aloud, "Are you happy to be back?"

There was no reply. Their silence was to be expected, and yet it worried him. He sensed that Mom was troubled about why his older sister, Rachel, hadn't yet arrived. And Dad seemed to have his doubts as to whether he'd see his own sister, Aunt Heather, again.

The man said, "They'll here soon. We'll all be together soon. I promise."

But he thought he heard a whisper in the air of all three of them asking...

"When?"

He gulped with shame and sorrow. He couldn't answer that question—at least not fully, and not yet. However, although he didn't dare make any promises, he did feel confident that he'd be able to bring Rachel here tomorrow.

But in his sister Mo's silence, the man detected another concern.

She doesn't like how I'm doing this.

She doesn't like that there's so much blood.

He almost said aloud to her...

"Don't worry, they don't feel any pain."

But was that really true? He'd struck the man and woman down quickly enough—before they'd even known it, he thought. Surely they'd not felt the knife severing their throats.

But the girl yesterday had only been dazed, not knocked fully unconscious.

She hadn't cried out when he'd delivered the fatal slash.

But her eyes.

Her eyes had been wide open. She'd known what was happening. She'd known what he was about to do to her. And she must have experienced at least a few moments of pain and terror before she died.

Did Mo know that? Did she maybe even carry some memory of that agony? If she did, it surely clouded any joy she might feel about the reunion that was underway.

I must do better for the next ones, he told himself.

All he wanted was for his family to be as perfect as it once was. He just needed to have them back again—and to stop feeling so guilty for how he'd lost them.

And he could feel, right here and now, that Mom, Dad, and Mo truly wanted for their whole family to be reunited. As tempted as he felt to make promises to their shadows at the table, he thought better of it.

I'll prove myself with actions, he told himself.

Not that the way ahead was at all clear to him. Although he'd found Rachel and had some idea of how he was going to approach her, he still had no idea when, how, or where he'd find Aunt Heather.

But maybe, he thought, that was as it should be.

Who ever said redemption should be easy?

His eventual success would be all the sweeter for having been hard-earned.

CHAPTER NINETEEN

As Riley parked the car, she got a tingling feeling about this visit to Joan Cornell's house. Yesterday, when she and Jenn had been here at the murdered woman's home, her instincts hadn't fully kicked in.

Today already seemed different.

For one thing, she was arriving alone …

Just like the killer did.

And this time she wouldn't be distracted by having to ask all her initial questions about the crime scene, or by having to explain her thoughts to anybody else.

Even Jenn could be a distraction, as she had been when they'd been here before and Riley had had to stop her from having an argument with Chief Shore. As disturbing as it was to have no idea of Jenn's whereabouts, Riley had to admit that it was just as well to be here alone this time.

Maybe she'd get a stronger feeling of the killer's presence.

Before driving away from Wolfe's Furniture to come here, she'd called Joan Cornell's daughter, Lori Tovar, to ask her whether her mother had kept a spare key hidden outside the house. Sure enough, there was such a key, and Lori had been glad to tell Riley where it was. And now, as Riley walked toward the house, she picked up a loose piece of stone from the low wall surrounding a carefully trimmed evergreen shrub and found the key exactly where it was supposed to be.

Then Riley ducked under the police tape that still blocked off the porch, walked up to the front door, unlocked it, and let herself inside.

She stood for a moment just looking around, keenly aware of the sheer emptiness of the place. She thought again of poor Lori's guilt about wanting this house to start a family with her husband, and how that dream was now shattered for her.

Riley wondered—who would wind up buying this place?

Of course, legally the buyers would have to be informed that there had been a murder here. Would that trouble the minds of prospective new owners? Or would they simply not care?

Riley sighed as she thought...

This might be a happy place again someday.

But right now, she thought that the house felt desolate, haunted by the terrible thing that had happened here. It might be a long time—if ever—before the dark cloud of Joan Cornell's murder lifted.

Still standing just inside the front door, Riley reminded herself of the task she was here for.

It was time for her to try to get a sense of the killer's mind. So far, any helpful information had eluded her.

Riley still didn't know exactly how the killer had gotten into the house. There had been no sign of forced entry. Perhaps he'd simply knocked on the front door and Joan had let him in. Then again, she might have left the door unlocked. After all, Joan had lived here for many years, ever since a time when one could leave one's door unlocked in a neighborhood like this.

Old habits die hard, Riley thought.

If so, the killer might have simply let himself inside, as Riley believed he had at Drew Cadigan's apartment.

But what had happened when he first came through the door?

Riley doubted that Joan and the killer had any prior relationship. But she also felt sure that he could exercise a fair amount of charm. Had Joan instinctively trusted him, at least at first?

Riley thought maybe so.

They talked for a moment, Riley thought.

He convinced her that he was here for some innocent reason.

And then...

Her eyes drifted over into the dining room area, where she noticed anew the empty spot at the table where the stolen chair had been.

The chair had obviously mattered to him ...

He noticed it right away.

Riley walked toward the table, picturing that a chair matching the other three chairs was still where it was supposed to be. As she had at Drew's apartment, she imagined the killer touching the chair, saying something about it to Joan.

And the same as she had at that other crime scene, Riley sensed that Joan found this to be an unsettling gesture.

So what did she do?

Riley looked over at the narrow counter that separated the dining room from the kitchen. The reddish splotch on the far side was still there, marking where the killer had smashed Joan's head against the hard marble.

Why had Joan gone over there behind the counter?

Riley remembered Jenn's speculation to Chief Shore ...

"Maybe he asked the victim for a glass of water."

But Riley now sensed that Jenn had been wrong. Joan had already grown suspicious of the killer, perhaps sensed the danger she was in, and had begun thinking about how she might be able to defend herself in case of an attack.

Of course! Riley realized.

Like any housewife, Joan knew that the kitchen was full of all kinds of potential weapons. She'd gone back there to find a knife or a rolling pin or something else she could defend herself with.

As Joan had headed back there, Riley guessed that she'd chattered nervously, trying to make conversation so as to not betray her rising suspicion. Maybe she'd tried to tell the killer that she was going into the kitchen to get him a drink or a snack.

But Riley was getting a stronger sense of the killer now, and she felt sure ...

He wasn't fooled.

And he hadn't been worried either.

In one swift, fell movement, he'd bounded over to the counter, reached across it and grabbed Joan by the hair, then smashed her head violently against the edge of the marble top.

And then?

Following in his footsteps, she stepped around the counter. The taped outline where the police had marked the position of the corpse was still on the floor. It was easy for Riley to imagine Joan's crumpled, unconscious body lying there.

It was also easy to imagine him seizing her by the hair again and pulling her head back and slashing her throat with a knife he'd brought with him for that purpose. But how had he felt when the blood had gushed from her wound and her windpipe had made hideous gurgling sounds?

Satisfied?

Elated?

Or had he felt simply nothing at all?

Perhaps the killing itself had been of no consequence to him.

After all, Riley knew he'd had some other purpose in mind all along.

Following in his footsteps again, she stepped away from where the dying body had lain and walked back over to the table. For some reason, the missing chair had been his real target all along, although Riley couldn't yet imagine why.

She pantomimed his movements, taking hold of the imaginary chair.

But what had he done then?

Riley remembered looking out over the backyard at Drew Cadigan's apartment house. She'd felt sure the killer had made his exit that way as he'd taken the chair with him.

She walked farther back into the house until she came to a back door with a window overlooking Joan's backyard. Sure enough, Riley could see an alley beyond the back fence. The same as at the apartment house, the killer could have had a vehicle waiting for him there. All he had to do was open this door and walk brazenly away…

Riley let out a dissatisfied sigh.

Her feeling of the killer had been quite strong, but now it was waning.

Her head was still full of unanswered questions.

Why? she wondered.

What had driven him to such a monstrous act—not once, but three times now?

And why had he stolen the chairs?

Riley still couldn't make sense of it.

She wondered if maybe she was going about things all wrong...

Maybe I rushed it.

And now she wondered if maybe *he* hadn't rushed through things at all. Perhaps he hadn't been in a hurry, hadn't simply grabbed the chair and made his escape with it.

Maybe he took his time.

Maybe he enjoyed the moment.

After all, what was the rush? Now that the woman was dead, might he not just wander around a bit, having a look at things?

Still imagining that she was following in the killer's footsteps, Riley walked back into the living room. This time her eye was caught by something odd in the glow of sunlight falling on a cluster of objects on the piano.

She stepped closer and saw the same group of framed family photographs she'd noticed here yesterday. But this time, Riley saw that light from the window was reflecting brightly off one spot in the midst of those pictures. Riley looked closely at the top of the piano and realized that it hadn't been dusted for a few days at least. Nevertheless, there was one dust-free spot that was catching the sunlight. From the shape of that area, Riley guessed that another picture had been here among the others until recently—perhaps until just the day before yesterday.

Riley felt her pulse quicken.

Did he steal a picture too?

She knew one way of finding out. Her cell phone now had a list of phone numbers for all the people she'd already interviewed about the case. She punched in the number for Lori Tovar, who quickly answered.

Riley explained to Lori that she had returned to her mother's house to pursue her investigation.

Then she said, "I was wondering—did you notice anything else that was missing from your mother's home other than her dining room chair?"

"Like what?" Lori asked.

"Well, like maybe one of the photographs from the top of her piano."

Lori fell quiet for a moment, then said...

"To be perfectly honest, I don't think I noticed one way or the other. Does it *look* like one of them is missing?"

"I think so," Riley said. "There's an empty space between two of them—one that looks like you graduating from high school, and another that seems to be of you and your siblings on a fishing trip."

Riley heard Lori gasp slightly.

"There *was* a picture there," Lori said. "It was a nice framed picture of Mom. Do you think the killer stole the picture too?"

Riley almost replied, *Yes, that's exactly what I think.*

But she stopped herself and told her instead, "I'm not ready to come to any conclusions. But you've been extremely helpful. Thank you."

Lori assured Riley that she'd be more than happy to answer any more questions, and they ended the call.

She stood in the living room for a moment with the phone in her hand. She sensed that a new pattern was starting to emerge. In this house, after this murder, a personal image had been taken along with a chair.

Had that happened after the other murders, too?

She had a powerful gut feeling that similar photos had been stolen from the other two crime scenes.

She closed her eyes and pictured the cluttered, untidy apartment that Drew had shared with her roommate, Sylvia. She could clearly remember that the refrigerator was covered with what amounted to a wild collage of photos, cartoons, notes, and fliers.

And if I'm right...

Nervous with excitement, Riley tapped Sylvia's number on her cell phone. When Sylvia answered, Riley asked her where she was at the moment. Luckily, Sylvia was right there studying in the apartment.

Riley said, "Sylvia, I need for you to look at all those pictures you've got on your refrigerator door. Can you tell if one of them is missing?"

Riley heard Sylvia's footsteps as she walked toward the refrigerator.

"Why, yes," she said after a few moments. "It's a photo of Drew that I took when we first moved in here together. I guess I hadn't noticed it was gone, there are so many others here. But what does it mean?"

Again, Riley refrained from offering any conclusions. She thanked Sylvia for her help and ended the call.

Two down, one to go, she thought.

Next she punched in the number for Ian Selves, the son of the man who had been murdered two weeks ago. When she got his message service, Riley said...

"Ian, I need to ask you a question. Is there a group of family pictures prominently displayed in your house? If so, does one picture happen to be missing? Please get back to me and let me know."

Riley guessed she might not hear back from Ian right away. He might not even know whether a picture was missing. He might have to wait until he had a break from classes and then check with his mother, who was probably at work. That could all take some time.

And yet it hardly seemed to matter.

Riley thought it was very likely that a picture had been stolen from the Selves house as well. But if she was right, what could the theft of those photos mean?

As she struggled to make sense of it, she flashed back to last night's dream—that image of the three murdered people seated at a dining room table in those stolen chairs...

Like at a family dinner.

Ever since she'd had that dream, she'd been sure that the killer was somehow obsessed with the concept of family. And now, the stolen pictures suggested that his obsession was quite specific—and deeply personal.

All this seemed to Riley like the beginning of some important insight. But she still couldn't quite make sense of it. She let out a discouraged groan.

Where the hell is Jenn?

Now that she'd had time to contemplate the scene alone, it would help to have someone to brainstorm with.

But then it occurred to her—there *was* someone she could talk with about all this.

And he had a keener grasp of human nature than just about anybody she'd ever known.

She got out her phone and started to punch in a familiar number.

CHAPTER TWENTY

Riley felt as though ghosts were breathing over her shoulder. The walls of Joan Cornell's uninhabited house seemed to be closing in on her. She stopped punching numbers into her phone. She knew she wasn't thinking very clearly, and she knew who she wanted to talk to about it.

But not from here, she thought.

She wanted to make a Skype call, but she needed to find some place where she could think and talk in peace. She remembered spotting a little park as she drove through Springett to get here. That would do.

As Riley left the house, she realized how badly this case was getting to her. Or maybe it was the combination of the case and the disappearance of her partner. Or maybe it was the absence of her usual partner, Bill Jeffreys.

Pull yourself together, she ordered. *People are getting killed.*

She left the house and drove to the park, which didn't seem to be crowded. She even saw a little gazebo that looked unoccupied.

As she parked her car and walked to the gazebo, Riley realized that this was a pleasant warm day. She hadn't even noticed before that the trees were bright with the reds and golds of fall. She'd been too immersed in her case to really look around.

But even now, she felt those confusing questions still tugging at her mind.

She sat down all alone and took out her computer tablet. She opened up her Skype program and put in a call.

Mike Nevins answered right away.

Riley felt relieved to see Mike's familiar, friendly face. He was a forensic psychiatrist who frequently consulted for the FBI, and he had helped Riley on many cases over the years. He'd helped her through a few personal problems as well, and she considered him to be a close friend.

Mike was sitting in his tidy office, immaculately groomed and dapperly dressed as usual in an expensive shirt and a vest. He flashed his charming smile and said in his gentle, purring voice…

"Hello there, Riley. I'd say it's a pleasure to see you, but I suspect you're not calling me for pleasure."

"I'm afraid not, Mike," Riley said.

Mike leaned back in his chair and said, "I've heard through the grapevine that you're in the Philly area investigating a serial killer there. How's it going?"

"That's what I need to talk to you about," Riley said.

Riley told him everything that had happened since she and Jenn had arrived in Philadelphia—everything, that is, except Jenn's mysterious disappearance. She emphasized the stolen furniture and photographs. She also told him about her dream.

Mike chuckled and said, "Dreams can be helpful things, can't they? It sounds like yours might have offered some insights. What do you think?"

Riley said, "It seems obvious to me that the killer is obsessed with family."

Mike nodded and said, "That seems obvious to me as well."

"Beyond that, I'm not sure what to think," Riley said.

Mike stroked his chin and said, "I assume you've tried to get into his mind. Have you had any success?"

"A little," Riley said. "Just now, at one of the crime scenes, I felt like I was able to walk through his actions, imagine how one of the murders unfolded. I could sense how he got into the victim's home, gained her trust, then attacked her, and—"

Mike gently interrupted, "But you're just talking about his actions, his *behaviors*. What kind of emotions did you pick up about him? What was he *feeling* when he killed those people?"

Riley felt a jolt of realization.

She'd known that something was missing from her attempts to connect with the killer.

And now she knew what it was ...

Feeling.

She admitted, "I'm afraid his emotions have been kind of a blank to me."

Mike tilted his head and said, "Well, you won't get very far into the why of all this until you get some idea of what he's been feeling, will you?"

Riley shrugged silently.

Of course she knew that Mike was right.

Mike stroked his chin for a moment, then said ...

"Tell me, Riley—since family is such an issue for him, what do you think *his* family life is like? Right now, I mean?"

Riley felt as though something vague was now coming into focus.

She said, "I—I can't imagine that he *has* a family."

Mike shrugged a little and said, "Well, he must have had a family at one time or another. We all do. We all come from somewhere. Even if he was an orphan, there must have been people in his life he thought of as family somehow. Where are they now?"

Riley felt a surprising chill as she was realized ...

I finally do feel a connection with him.

Right here and now.

With his usual clinical skill, Mike had managed to coax her into at least a slight, momentary bit of insight. And now she felt the hint of a profound, almost unfathomable loneliness, and she thought she knew what that meant.

"They're dead," she said. "His whole family is dead."

As Mike smiled knowingly, Riley hastily added, "Or at least I *think* they're dead. It's just a feeling, but ..."

"It's not *just* a feeling, Riley. It never is for you. Feelings are your most important talent, your rarest gift. Just do what you always do—follow your gut, see where your instincts take you."

Riley felt her sense of connection with the killer start to weaken. She wasn't surprised, since it had come on so unexpectedly. Even so, that wave of loneliness was still palpable.

Feeling a little confused now, she stammered...

"I—I'm not sure. Do you think he may have *murdered* his family?"

Mike chuckled again.

"Who am I to say? These are *your* instincts, Riley."

Riley shook her head, feeling very little connection at all now.

She said, "Maybe I'm having trouble because I've never worked on an actual familicide case. This summer down in Mississippi I worked on a case involving family annihilation, but the killer wasn't actually a member of the family he killed. This would be different. What drives someone to kill his own family?"

Mike's eyes crinkled thoughtfully.

He said, "Clinically, familicide involves four types of killers. The *anomic* killer is typically a well-to-do individual for whom his family is simply an extension of his prestige. When he faces financial ruin, his family loses the only status he sees in them, provoking him to kill them—and himself."

Riley turned the idea over in her head. Somehow she doubted that this killer was ever especially rich. At least, there had been no sign of that so far.

Mike continued, "The *disappointed* killer acts out of rage, a feeling that his family is inadequate and has let him down in some terrible way. The *self-righteous* killer is acting out of some sort of perceived wrong—for example, a divorced man who believes his ex-wife has turned his children against him. He punishes the wife by killing their children."

Riley shook her head slightly. Those two types of killers didn't ring right to her either.

Mike said, "Finally, there's the *paranoid* killer. He kills his family out of some twisted desire to protect them from some dire, imagined threat."

Riley squinted with thought.

"That *might* be it," she said. "I get the feeling that he's definitely out of touch with reality. He might even have thought he was doing his family a favor if he killed them. But my strongest impression ..."

Riley paused, trying to put her thought into words. Again, she remembered that dining room table in her dream, where the corpses seemed to be posed as if at a family dinner.

"He's a *collector*, Mike. He collects chairs and portraits, but his obsession goes much deeper than that."

"Like he's *collecting* family members?" Mike suggested.

Riley said, "More like he's trying to put his lost family back together, as if he thinks all he has to do is find them and gather them up."

Mike crossed his arms and said, "That could involve powerful feelings of guilt. Do you sense that he's acting somehow out of guilt?"

Riley's scalp tingled at this idea.

"Yes, I think so," she said. "Guilt is the emotion I've been having trouble putting my finger on. I'm getting the sense that his dominant emotions are guilt and loneliness."

Mike nodded and said, "It makes sense. I ought to mention one other thing about familicidal killers. About half of them wind up killing themselves. The killer you're after hasn't done that—at least not yet. Even so, he's likely to be carrying around a staggering load of guilt."

Her eyes widening with interest, Riley said, "Which means he's channeled his guilt away from suicide."

Mike leaned forward a little and said, "That's right. And it must take tremendous effort. Through it all, he's living in a psychic 'perfect storm' of loneliness and guilt—and probably unresolved and pent-up rage."

Starting to see what Mike was getting at, Riley said, "And that means ..."

Her voice trailed off, and Mike finished her thought.

"Which means he's *extremely* dangerous. More so than you've probably reckoned on. I hope you're working with a solid and dependable partner. You'll both need to watch each other's back."

Riley slumped a little.

Should I tell him about Jenn? she wondered.

Seeming to sense Riley's unease, Mike said, "I get the feeling that there are one or two things you're not telling me."

Riley nodded silently.

"Would you like to get them out in the open?" Mike said.

Riley shook her head.

Mike smiled a warm, kindly smile.

"Well, that's up to you, Riley," he said. "It's always up to you. I'm always here if you need me. My door's always open, both figuratively and literally. I hope you know that."

"Thanks, Mike," Riley said. "And thanks for all your help just now."

Riley was about to end the call when Mike added...

"Oh, there's one other thing I think you should keep in mind. People don't always feel guilty over things they've done wrong. They can even feel guilty over things they were never really responsible for."

"I'm not sure I understand," Riley said.

Mike chuckled and said, "I'm not sure I do either. I've don't know whether that idea applies to your case at all, but...well, it's something you might need to consider."

Riley thanked him again, and they ended the chat session.

Riley sat in the gazebo wondering exactly why she hadn't told him about Jenn's mysterious absence. She could think of one good reason. She didn't want to involve Mike in her own rule-breaking behavior, make him an accomplice in any way. She knew he would keep any secret she told him, but she didn't want to put him in a compromising position.

She heaved a long, melancholy sigh.

Good old Mike, she thought.

She knew she could take him at his word that his door was always open—and not just over forensic matters. She figured she needed to have a good talk with him when this case was over. He could help her deal with a lot of the emotional stuff that was troubling her these days, especially her issues of trust with friends and loved ones.

Meanwhile, she had a case to solve. And as of right now, it looked like she might have to solve it alone. She felt that her conversation with Mike had been productive, although one thing he'd said rather puzzled her…

"People don't always feel guilty over things they've done wrong. They can feel guilty over things they were never really responsible for."

She wondered—what might that have to do with the murderer she was hunting right now? After all, he truly was guilty in deed as well as thought. He'd killed three people that Riley knew of— and now she was convinced that he'd killed his own family as well. Surely any guilt he felt was fraught with a very real sense of personal responsibility.

She quickly decided it was just an idle thought on Mike's part. She also knew what her next course of action should be.

She got out her cell phone and called Chief Shore.

When he answered, Riley said, "I've got reason to believe that our killer once killed members of his own family—maybe all of them. I was wondering if you could run a search of unsolved family annihilation cases in the area and—"

The chief interrupted, "Holy shit. I know who it is."

Riley stifled a gasp of surprise.

"What do you mean?" she said.

"I don't have time to explain," Shore said. "I'm going to give you an address to drive to. I'll meet you there—and with some luck I'll already have an arrest warrant. But before you go, get on your computer and Google the name 'Leonard Robbins' with the words 'family' and 'homicide.' See what comes up."

Chief Shore ended the call without another word.

Riley sat staring at her phone for a moment, wondering what to make of what the chief had just said.

All she knew was that things suddenly seemed to be moving fast.

Maybe too fast.

CHAPTER TWENTY ONE

Riley felt a little dizzy as she made the search on her computer tablet. Just moments ago, she had been Skyping with Mike Nevins, theorizing and speculating about what might be driving the killer. Any solution to the case had seemed elusive.

But now...

Her Google search for the name "Leonard Robbins" with the words "family" and "homicide" was yielding some interesting local news items.

She thought maybe Chief Shore was right—that this was the killer and they'd have him in custody very soon.

A young man named Leonard Robbins, the heir to a prosperous construction company here in Springett, had once been arrested and charged with murdering his immediate family—his father, mother, and sister.

She was looking for a family killer who for some twisted reason hadn't been able to stop with his own family. This could be the one.

A couple of years ago, Rudolph Robbins, his wife, May, and his daughter, Nisha, were all killed in their van in a fatal accident on a busy highway that passed through Springett. The police, led by Chief Shore himself, were convinced that the van's brakes had been tampered with.

Leonard Robbins had seemed a likely suspect. He had been kicked out of several Ivy League universities, abused drugs and alcohol, and was a disappointment to his parents. According to several family acquaintances, Rudolph Robbins had planned to cut Leonard out of his will.

The accident had occurred just in time to keep that from happening.

When the police found tools in Leonard's possession that could have been used to tamper with the vehicle's brakes, Chief Shore arrested him right away. Unfortunately for Shore and the prosecutors, forensic experts gave contradicting reports as to whether the van's brakes had really been tampered with or not. All charges were soon dropped.

Riley's eyes darted over the small screen as she skimmed the articles. Striking details jumped out at her—for example, the ages of the dead family members. Rudolph Robbins had been fifty-four years old, his wife fifty-two, and his daughter nineteen—all of them close to the ages of the recent murder victims.

Riley could certainly see why Chief Shore thought Leonard Robbins might be the killer they were looking for.

More than that, she could understand why Shore *wanted* that to be true.

But Riley knew from hard experience that wanting something to be true and proving it were two different things. Was Chief Shore jumping to conclusions? And how on earth did he expect to get a warrant so quickly?

All Riley knew for sure was that she'd better head straight for the address Shore had given her. But just as she started out of the gazebo toward her car, her phone buzzed.

She had a text message from Ian Selves that read...

On my way to class so can't talk now. But thought you should know right away that I called Mom and she says there is a photo of Dad missing from our mantel. She thought I'd taken it for my dorm room to remember Dad by. I didn't. Hope this helps. Call if you need anything else.

Riley stood on the gazebo steps, processing this new information. She'd suspected, of course, that a picture had been stolen from the Selves household. Now her suspicion was confirmed...

This killer is a collector, all right.

Obviously he was collecting furniture and photos, and that only made sense if he was collecting more than just things. She felt more certain than ever about that.

This killer was trying to collect his lost family.

It seemed possible that Leonard Robbins would fit the profile that was shaping in her mind. Even so, it occurred to her that maybe it didn't matter—not if Chief Shore had Robbins dead to rights. Riley's work here in Springett might come to an end sooner than she'd expected.

She'd be perfectly happy if things turned out that way. Still, it would feel strange to solve this case with Jenn still missing. And what would she say in her report to Meredith about Jenn's absence?

Where is she anyway? Riley wondered.

She hoped that later today she would have some time to start seriously tracking Jenn down. But right now, there was a murder suspect to apprehend. She walked to the borrowed car and drove away from the peaceful little park.

Minutes later Riley found herself in the most expensive neighborhood she'd been to so far in Springett. The address was for a broad, luxurious Colonial-style house situated on a spacious and perfectly kept lawn.

As she pulled into the curved drive in front of the house, Riley saw a police van arriving from the opposite direction. The vehicle stopped, and Chief Shore got out with three uniformed cops. They were well-armed and wearing Kevlar vests.

Definitely ready for trouble, Riley realized.

Wearing a vest himself, Chief Shore strode toward Riley with a cheerful smile.

"Did you find the information I told you about, Agent Paige?"

"I did," Riley said.

"Well then, you know what we're dealing with," Chief Shore said. Where's your partner?"

Riley swallowed hard and said, "She's working elsewhere."

She hated to lie. But she felt pretty sure this wasn't the last lie she was going to have to tell on Jenn's behalf.

Shore shrugged and said, "Well, it's too bad she's going to have to miss this."

He pulled out an arrest warrant and showed it to her.

"Anyway, we're good to go," he said. "Are you ready to shut the lid on this case, Agent Paige?"

Riley squinted at the paper in his hand.

"How did you get a warrant so fast?" she asked.

Or at all? she wondered, without saying so aloud.

The case for arresting Leonard Robbins struck her as flimsy at best.

"Judge Knight doesn't like to waste time," Chief Shore said with a chuckle. "And he doesn't like unfinished business, if you know what I mean."

Riley nodded. She was starting to understand the situation better. She remembered the judge's name from the news articles she'd just read. He'd been the judge who had reluctantly dismissed the case against Leonard Robbins.

It was obvious to Riley that Judge Knight and Chief Shore were on friendly terms. More than that, they shared a mutual grudge over how the case against Robbins had turned out. Judge Knight had apparently been more than happy to process the warrant right away.

All this made Riley feel a little uneasy. She'd learned that local police sometimes made mistakes when grudges were involved. She hoped that wasn't the case this time.

Chief Shore looked at the large house and commented, "That's where Leonard Robbins lives—all alone, now that his family's dead. There's a good chance we'll catch him at home. He's not going to be happy to see us, though."

He looked Riley over and added, "You look a little underdressed for the occasion. I've got another vest in the van if you want it."

Riley shook her head. Somehow, this didn't strike her as a situation in which firearms would come into play.

"Suit yourself," Shore said. "You might want to hang back when my men and I arrest him, though. Don't put yourself in unnecessary danger."

Riley nodded and followed Shore toward the house. She thought the chief seemed almost weirdly relaxed and casual. He hardly seemed to be expecting any danger, despite being well prepared for it.

As they walked, Shore commented, "A little while ago I got an interesting call from a couple of female employees at Wolfe's Furniture. They said you'd told them to get in touch with me. Something about their boss peeking at them in the employee restroom, is that right?"

Riley nodded and said, "That's right. The women will be able to give you open-and-shut evidence of invasion of privacy. There's also a long history of sexual harassment involved. This Cassius Wolfe guy's a real bastard. It's high time for him to be stopped for good."

Shore chuckled and said, "Well, with a little bit of luck, I'll be able to get to that later today."

As they neared the house, Riley saw that Shore and his three men had their hands near their weapons. Obeying the chief's suggestion, she stayed at the rear. She really didn't think that her own presence was much needed…

It's their arrest to make.

And from what Riley knew about the situation, they'd want to savor the opportunity.

Riley and the four men stepped onto the front portico, and Shore knocked on the door. A dark-skinned woman with a Spanish accent answered the door. Shore told her he was here to see Leonard Robbins.

At that moment, one of Shore's cops yelped, "I see him!"

Riley saw him too. He was coming down a flight of stairs that featured an elegant curving banister. At the sight of the cops, he froze on the stairs like a proverbial deer in headlights.

In a split second, Leonard Robbins made a strong impression on Riley—and it wasn't a good impression. He was wearing a preppy-looking polo shirt, and he had thick, exquisitely coiffed brown hair and a babyish face. She'd seen his type before—spoiled, privileged, and probably narcissistic.

She had an instant gut feeling that this man really had killed someone—his own family, at least. It now seemed no wonder to her that Shore and his cops and even the judge were eager to nail him once and for all.

The cops pushed their way into the hallway, and the woman who had answered the door scurried quietly away. As one of the cops moved toward him, Leonard darted the rest of the way down the stairs, then wheeled and broke into a run down an adjoining hallway.

"Get him!" Shore yelled.

The three cops easily caught up with the fleeing man. The cop who had first noticed Robbins twisted his arm behind his back while another cop whipped out a pair of handcuffs.

The suspect writhed and twisted and yelled...

"Let me go! Let me go! What the hell is this all about anyway? What do you think you're doing?"

The cop who was trying to subdue him smiled back at Chief Shore and called out...

"He's quite a handful, Chief."

Chief Shore crossed his arms and replied, "I can see that. Well, do whatever you have to do."

The cop seemed to take that as permission to get considerably rougher. He wrestled Leonard to a nearby side table and slammed him face down against it, then lifted his head and slammed it down again.

Riley cringed at what was obviously unnecessary force.

And yet she couldn't help thinking...

I've got no right to judge.

After all, just yesterday she had let her own rage get the best of her while apprehending Tony Moore at the LangMart store—rage that she hadn't even felt toward him personally. She figured Shore and his men at least had good reason for hating this jerk.

147

While the cop who had subdued Leonard held him against the table, another cop put the handcuffs on him.

Chief Shore walked over beside the suspect and said in a mock-friendly tone…

"It's nice to see you again, Robbins. I hope the feeling is mutual."

"What do you think you're doing?" Leonard said, his voice muffled because his head lay squashed sideways on the table.

"You're under arrest, friend," Shore said. "For the murders of Justin Selves, Joan Cornell, and Drew Cadigan."

"I've never heard of them," Leonard said.

Shore said, "No? We'll have to see about that."

As Shore read Leonard his rights, Riley glanced around the house. It was a beautiful place, spacious and tastefully decorated. Even though it was way too big and ostentatious for her liking, it wasn't pretentious like many rich people's homes she'd been inside. Across a nearby room, a pair of French doors led to a patio, a swimming pool, and a lawn that spread out for a long distance.

Riley thought about where this luxury must have come from. The news articles had mentioned that the Robbins family owned a construction company. At one time or another, at least one member of the family had put in a lot of hard work to acquire all this wealth.

And now just one person lived here all by himself—this pampered punk who had probably murdered his own family.

It's a shame, Riley thought.

It certainly seemed small wonder to her that that Leonard's parents had been disappointed in him. But they had apparently paid a fatal price for their disappointment.

As she had at Joan Cornell's house, Riley wondered—what was going to become of this house now? Who was going to wind up owning it? What kind of people would they be? Would they be troubled that a probable murderer had once lived here?

She only hoped that Leonard wouldn't get off free again and spend the rest of his days in comfort here.

She followed Chief Shore and his men as they escorted Leonard Robbins to their van and pushed him roughly inside. Getting into the driver's seat, Chief Shore called out to Riley, "We'll meet you at the station."

Riley nodded, then got into her borrowed car.

As she started the engine, she tried to shake the feeling that something wasn't quite right about this arrest.

It wasn't that Leonard Robbins was innocent, but there had been something in his tone when Shore mentioned the names of the recently murdered people.

"I've never heard of them."

Of course, it was exactly what she'd expected him to say.

And yet she wondered…

Did he mean it?

CHAPTER TWENTY TWO

A short time later, Riley stood staring at the man they had just arrested for murder. Watching through the two-way mirror at the Springett police station, she found it easy to believe that he had killed his own family—all of them, and out of simple greed. She was trying to determine whether those had been his only victims.

Had he enjoyed the murders so much that he hadn't wanted to stop? Or could some dark form of guilt have driven him to kill several strangers?

Inside the interrogation room, Leonard Robbins was in handcuffs, sitting at a gray table. Staring down at the tabletop, he muttered yet again, "I'm not saying anything until my lawyer gets here."

Chief Shore was pacing back and forth in front of him.

"That's fine," Shore said in a casual tone of voice. "You've got a right to remain silent. But I've also got a right to keep asking you questions, don't I?"

This had been going on for a few minutes now. Leonard kept saying he wouldn't talk without his lawyer present, and Shore kept badgering him with questions anyway—weird, almost nonsensical questions that Riley knew had no real purpose except to throw the suspect hopelessly off balance.

Riley had to admit that she was impressed by Shore's style and skill.

He's one hell of an interrogator.

In fact, she doubted whether she could handle this better herself.

Right now Shore was asking Leonard whether he really lived alone in that big house he'd inherited. She knew the question really had nothing to do with the case—but of course, that was exactly the point as far as Shore was concerned. Leonard was growing more confused and flustered by the moment. Although he knew he shouldn't talk, he couldn't seem to stop himself from babbling incoherent replies.

With some luck, Riley figured Shore would get a confession out of him before his lawyer even got here.

But a confession to what?

Riley now felt almost positive that Leonard had killed his family.

But what about the three recent victims—Justin Selves, Joan Cornell, and Drew Cadigan?

Riley wasn't so sure about that. She thought back to her conversation with Mike Nevins shortly before the arrest, and the hypotheses they'd formed about the killer—for example, that he was consumed by guilt.

She remembered what Mike had said...

"Through it all, he's living in a psychic 'perfect storm' of loneliness and guilt—and probably unresolved and pent-up rage."

Looking at Leonard Robbins right now, Riley didn't sense any of those emotions. But she also knew that there were possibilities that she and Mike hadn't discussed.

One was that he had simply gone insane.

The man in the interrogation room was probably incapable of morality, much less guilt. But it was easy for Riley to see that he was a *weak* man. Killing his own family might be the only serious thing he'd ever accomplished in his useless life. He'd probably been quite proud of himself for a short time afterward.

But then maybe he hadn't reckoned on the ongoing fortitude it would take to keep his awful secret. Living every day with the fear of getting caught might well have proven to be too big a task for such a puny little man.

Maybe, Riley thought, his mind had finally cracked from sheer exhaustion. Maybe he'd lost touch with reality, and was now blindly pursuing and killing people out of some crazed attempt to deal with his terror.

It's possible, Riley thought.

But if it were true, what about the stolen photos and chairs? The team that had raided his house hadn't seen any sign of those, but their search had been cursory so far, and the things could have been kept elsewhere. They might still turn up.

The real problem was that Leonard Shore didn't seem to fit her gut feeling that the killer was obsessively trying to "collect" his family back together. How would those strange thefts fit into his personal breakdown?

Riley didn't know, and it bothered her.

Meanwhile, Chief Shore was steering his questioning in a dramatic new direction.

He opened a folder and spread some photographs across the table in front of the suspect—crime scene photos of the three slain victims with their throats cut.

Shore said to him with sharp sarcasm, "I guess I don't have to introduce you to these people, do I?"

Leonard's eyes widened and his mouth dropped open.

He let out a hoarse outcry, but he seemed unable to speak.

"Nothing to say?" Shore said. "Well, I wish you'd help me out. Their names have slipped my mind. I was hoping you could refresh my memory."

Leonard gasped and finally forced out some words.

"I don't know these people. I've never seen them before."

Shore said, "No? Well, think harder, OK? I'm sure you recognize them."

Leonard shook his head and said, "This is crazy."

Shore snapped his fingers and said, "Oh, *now* I remember their names!"

Shore pushed the pictures toward him one by one.

"This is Justin Selves, killed about two weeks ago. This is Joan Cornell, killed the day before yesterday. This is Drew Cadigan, murdered just yesterday."

From his face alone, it was easy for Riley to see what Leonard was feeling.

It's sheer exhaustion, she realized.

In a monotone, Leonard said, "I don't know anything about these people."

Riley remembered hearing Leonard say the same thing back when they'd arrested him. And once again she wondered…

Does he mean it?

Chief Shore barked, "Are you trying to tell me you didn't kill them, just like you killed your dad and mom and sister? Because that's sure as hell what I'm going to charge you with."

"This isn't the same thing," Leonard said.

"The same thing as what?" Shore said.

"It's not the same," Leonard repeated.

Riley's breath quickened. She sensed that Leonard was on the verge of snapping once and for all.

Shore leaned across the table and said, "How is it different?"

"I didn't cut anybody's throats," Leonard said.

"Is that right?" Shore said. "You're not saying you didn't kill anybody."

Leonard's body slumped in his chair. Riley was almost sure she saw him nod almost imperceptibly. For a moment, she thought he was about to confess.

Then he said, "I'm tired of this. I'm just really tired of this."

As Shore demanded to know just what Leonard was tired of, Riley heard a voice speak sharply behind her.

"What the hell is going on in there?"

Riley turned and saw a well-dressed man with a suitcase standing right behind her. She knew at a glance that he was Leonard Robbins's lawyer. And judging from his red-faced expression, he was seriously angry.

He pointed to what was going on beyond the two-way mirror and asked, "Is Shore interrogating my client?"

Riley shrugged slightly and said, "Your client knows his rights. Chief Shore is doing everything by the book."

"Really?" the lawyer said. "And who might you be?"

Riley produced her badge and introduced herself.

The lawyer squinted at her and said, "The FBI. Jesus. Why is this any of your business anyway?"

Without giving Riley a chance to answer, the lawyer charged into the interrogation room and hotly demanded that Chief Shore get away from his client. Shore just folded his arms and spoke softly and patiently while the lawyer kept ranting and jabbing his finger at his chest. Leonard Robbins sat slumped in his chair, looking hopeless and defeated.

As Riley watched the scene unfold among the three men, she realized...

There's a lot of history here.

These three men had all acted out much the same scene before—perhaps a good many times. Chief Shore had used any excuse or pretense to bring Leonard Robbins in for questioning, even if it was only for a speeding ticket or disturbing the peace. His only real reason for doing so was to wear Leonard down until he confessed to killing his family.

And now it looked like that might be about to happen.

Finally, Shore shrugged and left the room and joined Riley behind the mirror. He and Riley stood trying to hear what the lawyer and Leonard were saying in hushed voices. They managed to make out some important words.

"I can't do this anymore," Leonard said.

"As your attorney, I can't allow—" the lawyer said.

"It's my choice," Leonard said, interrupting.

"Leonard, I can't believe you want to—"

"It's not up to you."

The lawyer kept arguing with Leonard, but Riley could see that his objections were half-hearted.

I guess he's tired of all this too, she thought.

She'd been around enough defense attorneys during her career to know they took no great pleasure in defending guilty people. This one had probably had enough and would be relieved to have this whole thing over with once and for all.

And now Riley felt as though she understood exactly what was going on here.

Riley glanced over at Chief Shore and said, "Congratulations. It looks like he's going to confess."

"It does indeed," Shore said.

Riley said, "Too bad he's not going to confess to the three killings of the last couple of weeks."

"Why do you say that?" Shore said.

"Because he didn't commit them," Riley said.

"You don't think so?"

"I'm sure of it," Riley said.

Shore looked at her skeptically and said, "Well, I'll be damned if I don't think we've got the right man for all the murders. But if you don't think so, I guess that means you've still got your work cut out for you, doesn't it?"

Riley stood staring at Shore as he kept looking through the mirror. She couldn't help feeling angry. Without apparently meaning to, Shore had dragged her away on a detour.

And during the whole time since they'd been dealing with Leonard Robbins, a different murderer was still at large, probably getting ready to kill again...

If he hasn't already.

Riley was about to give voice to her complaints when the lawyer came out of the interrogation room with a look of resignation on his face.

He said to Chief Shore, "My client has something he wants to say to you."

Shore rubbed his hands together and said, "I'll bet he does. Let's get to it."

Shore and the lawyer went back into the room together. There was no doubt in Riley's mind that Leonard Robbins was about to make a full confession—but not to the murders that really concerned her. She still had a killer to track.

She didn't feel anywhere close to success.

As she stood in the little booth waiting to hear whatever was about to happen in the interrogation room, her phone rang. When she saw that the call was from Brent Meredith at Quantico, her gut told her that this wasn't going to be a pleasant conversation.

She stepped into the hallway and took the call.

She heard Meredith's voice rumble angrily, "Agent Paige, is there something you'd like to tell me?"

Oh, God, Riley thought. *He knows about Jenn.*

CHAPTER TWENTY THREE

Riley recognized the fury in Brent Meredith's voice. She'd heard that anger before—though never without good reason, at least as far as she was concerned. But now there was an unusual tension in his words.

She realized that her boss was struggling to control what he was saying.

That meant he was even angrier than usual.

She almost replied, *"What do you mean, sir?"*

Then Riley brushed aside any thoughts of evading his question, of maybe trying to bluff her way out of this.

In a halting voice she told him, "Sir, Agent Roston is missing."

"As of when?" Meredith said.

"I'm not sure. Sometime last night, I think. She wasn't in her hotel room this morning when I went to look for her. She didn't give me any warning."

Riley remembered the cryptic note she'd found on the nightstand...

Riley,
I'm sorry.
Jenn

She wondered—should she mention that to Meredith?

As she wavered, Meredith asked, "Do you have any idea where she might have gone?"

"I've got no idea, sir," Riley said.

She felt vaguely relieved to be able to tell the simple truth about that, at least.

Meredith growled, "Well, wherever she is, it doesn't sound like she has any intention of coming back."

"Not coming back?" Riley echoed, startled that Meredith seemed to know something she didn't.

"She didn't say anything to you about that?" Meredith asked.

"No, she sure didn't."

Meredith was silent for a long moment, then he said, "I just received an email from Roston. A letter was attached to it."

Riley choked back her questions and Meredith continued, "The letter says, 'I, Special Agent Jenn Roston, hereby submit my resignation from the FBI. It has been an honor to serve in such a fine and noble institution. But I believe I am no longer able to discharge my duties in a manner worthy of a BAU agent.'"

Meredith grunted and added, "The letter ends, 'Sincerely yours, Jennifer Roston.' No further explanation. I'm hoping you can help me make sense of this."

Riley realized her knees were shaking from the shock of what she was hearing. She'd assumed that Jenn was having some personal problem and would get it straightened out and be back on the job. They had both encountered issues like that in the past. They had both covered for each other. Of course, neither had left the other in the dark like this about what they were doing.

She stammered, "I—I don't know what to say."

"The truth would help," Meredith said. "How long has Roston been thinking about this move?"

"She didn't tell me anything about it, sir."

"No?" Meredith said. "I find that surprising. In my days in the field, partners knew everything about each other, including their deepest, darkest secrets. My own partners knew things about me that neither of my wives ever found out about. To the best of my knowledge, field agents still work that way. Are you trying to tell me you're the sole exception?"

Riley swallowed hard and said, "I assure you, I had no idea she was going to do this."

"I wish I could believe you," Meredith said. "But that's a little hard for me at the moment. You should have gotten in touch with me first thing this morning, the minute you knew your partner was missing. Now the day is almost over. Did you ever have any intention of telling me?"

Riley didn't know what to say.

The truth was, she really didn't know.

Did I ever intend to tell him?

She'd been hoping it would never be necessary.

Meredith's voice grew quieter, but still quavered with anger.

"I've got another problem. I've got a resignation letter, but what I don't have are a badge and a gun. She wouldn't have happened to leave those with you, would she?"

The question meant that Meredith still didn't believe her. He still thought she knew something about Jenn's disappearance.

She realized how severely she had damaged her relationship with her boss.

"No, sir," she replied firmly. "I'm afraid she didn't."

"This is bad, Agent Paige. This is very bad."

"I know," Riley said. "And I'll get right to work trying to find her."

"You'll do no such thing, damn it. I'll put our forensic technicians to work on that. You've still got a case to solve. How is that going, anyway?"

Riley stifled a sigh. There wasn't going to be a thing about this call that wasn't horrible.

"We just arrested a suspect," Riley said. "But I don't think he committed the murders we're investigating."

"Are you sure?"

Riley paused for a moment to wonder…

Am I sure?

Then she remembered that Chief Shore had all but admitted that he knew Leonard Robbins wasn't the recent killer.

"I guess that means you've still got your work cut out for you, doesn't it?"

Riley gulped and said in shaky voice, "I'm sure, sir."

"So your case is stalled?"

"The lead turned out to be a dead end," Riley admitted.

"Do you have any others?"

"Not right now."

Meredith snorted. "I expect that to change. You need to get this case moving by tomorrow or I'm putting a different team on it. And I want to see a thorough report about your methods, mistakes and all. Do you understand?"

"Yes, sir," Riley said. "I'm sorry, sir."

Silence fell again.

Then Meredith snapped, "Get back to work."

He ended the call without saying another word.

Riley stood in the police station hallway, leaning against a wall for support. Her mind was reeling from all that Meredith had just told her.

Jenn resigned, she thought. *But she didn't turn in her gun or her badge.*

What did that mean? Where had Jenn gone, and what might she be up to? Riley had no idea.

But she did know one thing. She hadn't told Meredith the whole truth. How could she even begin to do that?

She sighed as she remembered Meredith saying...

"My own partners knew things about me that neither of my wives ever found out about."

Whatever secrets Meredith may have been talking about, she doubted that they could compare with the dark secrets she and Jenn had shared. Jenn, after all, was the only person who knew the whole truth about Riley's twisted entanglement with the master criminal Shane Hatcher—an entanglement that had finally come to a violent end just last spring.

If Meredith had ever found out the truth about that relationship, it would have ended her career.

And of course, Riley knew everything about Jenn's relationship with Aunt Cora...

Or do I know everything?

Maybe not. Riley had no idea whether Jenn had fallen back into the criminal network of her one-time mentor. The fact that Jenn hadn't turned in her gun and her badge was a sobering thought. Jenn could be a great service to Aunt Cora if she could convincingly pass herself off as an FBI agent.

Riley was almost in tears now.

Brent Meredith had always been a good, fair boss, and had even stood up for her when she might not have even deserved it.

But all that was probably over.

She knew that Meredith would have to hand Jenn's letter over to his own superior, Special Agent in Charge Carl Walder. When he did, he'd surely tell Walder about Riley's failure to report Jenn's absence.

How could he not tell him?

Riley groaned under her breath as she remembered her past dealings with the baby-faced, bureaucratic Carl Walder. He'd always despised her, and the feeling was certainly mutual.

Walder had also fired or suspended Riley a handful of times, always with obvious glee. He was sure to do it again, and Riley knew she couldn't count on Meredith to come to her rescue.

In fact, it might be Meredith, not Walder, doing the firing this time. He had excellent reasons, after all—especially his personal disappointment in Riley's behavior.

It was a hopeless situation. And there was nothing Riley could do about it.

She stood straight again and reminded herself...

I still have a job to do.

It was probably the last case she'd ever have to solve for the BAU, but the least she could do was to finish it with her best skills and professionalism.

For the time being, though, it looked like she was going to have go it alone, without even any help from Chief Shore for the time being.

Meanwhile, people were walking past her gawking at her as she stood in the hallway. She felt like she had to get out of this police station or go completely crazy. She walked to the front entrance, only to be horrified by what she saw outside the glass doors.

A crowd of reporters was gathered on the front steps, wielding cell phones and cameras and microphones. As soon as they glimpsed her through the door, they started pounding on the glass.

Riley almost turned to flee back into the building.

No, I've got to face them, she realized.

She walked out the door, where she was buffeted from all sides by reporters.

They started shouting at her.

"Are you Special Agent Riley Paige?"

"Is it true that the BAU is now working on the case of the recent serial killings?"

Riley was rattled, and for a moment she wondered how they knew who she was. She quickly reminded herself that her name was well known in law enforcement circles—and by journalists as well. This bunch had simply done their jobs and had probably tracked down a photo of her.

Having no other choice, she flashed her badge and identified herself.

"I've got no comment to make at this time," she said.

She tried to push her way through the group, but the reporters were stubborn and swarmed even tighter around her.

"Is it true you've got a suspect in custody?" yelled one reporter.

"I've got no comment," Riley yelled back.

Another yelled, "Surely you can just give us an answer—yes or no."

Riley couldn't imagine what she could possibly say. It wasn't a question she could answer with a simple yes or no. Her frustration was starting to turn into anger now. Chief Shore had put her in a ridiculous situation. But now it occurred to her—maybe she could turn the tables on him.

She shouted, "Chief Shore will be making an announcement shortly."

Shouted questions kept coming, but less loudly and determinedly. At least some of the reporters seemed content with what she'd just said. She couldn't help smiling with satisfaction as the pressure around her ebbed and she was able to squeeze her way through the crowd.

Chief Shore didn't yet know it, but Riley had just scheduled a press conference for him.

She made her way to the borrowed car and got in and started driving. At first she didn't have a destination in mind. All she wanted was to get away from here as quickly as possible. But dusk was now setting in, and she decided to head straight back to her hotel. There she could collect her thoughts and decide on a course of action for tomorrow.

As she drove, she struggled to imagine whatever had happened to Jenn. She wished she could devote herself to tracking her partner down, starting right this minute. But Meredith had specifically ordered her not to do that. And the last thing she wanted to do right now was defy Meredith's instructions.

Keep your mind on the case, she told herself.

But she couldn't focus. The events of the last few hours had disrupted any progress she'd thought she was making. It now seemed as though she'd have to start from scratch.

And where do I begin? she wondered.

As she neared her hotel, she spotted a liquor store just ahead.

Maybe a drink or two is just what I need, she thought.

At least it would slow down her thoughts, calm the mental jangling that was besetting her right now. It might just make it possible for her to think through her next course of action.

She parked in front of the liquor store, walked inside, and bought a bottle of bourbon. Then she got back into the car and went straight to her hotel.

As she lugged the bottle to her room, Riley wondered...

Why did I buy a whole fifth of whiskey?

She'd done it without thinking. But she told herself it really didn't matter. She'd have one or two drinks this evening, then decide what to do with the rest of the bourbon tomorrow. She might take it back home with her on the plane after she finished this case. Or she might just leave it in the hotel room for someone else to enjoy, probably some underpaid maid.

Riley went into her room, poured herself a glass of whiskey, and sat down at the table.

She took a sip of the whiskey. The familiar burning sensation in her throat was comforting.

She checked her cell phone. There were no texts or messages from home. She wondered whether she should try to call April and Jilly, just to find out how they were and to let them know how she was doing.

But she remembered last night's call, all the fretting and complaining she'd gotten from both of the girls.

They're probably still mad at me, she thought.

And one thing she didn't need right now was anything to make her feel any worse than she already did.

Riley decided that the thing to do was to focus on the case. She got out her computer tablet and turned it on.

She thought back to her conversation with Mike Nevins. By the time they'd finished talking, she'd felt sure they were making progress. Of course, that progress had been disrupted by the arrest of Leonard Robbins.

But now it occurred to her that nothing had happened since that conversation to contradict the theories she and Mike had started to form. She thought back over her conversation with Mike, reviewing all their thoughts about the killer.

They'd both considered it very likely that he'd killed his own family at one time or another. And now, consumed by guilt and grief and loneliness, he was trying to replace them in his own insane, twisted way.

Leonard Robbins hadn't fit their profile, but somebody else out there probably did.

Maybe I don't really have to start from scratch, she thought.

After all, she had no reason to suppose that Leonard Robbins had committed the sole act of familicide in this area. Maybe she could find other cases and track down some new suspects.

She set to work Googling, trying to find cases of family annihilation in the Philadelphia area during the last couple of decades. She found only two. And in both of those cases, the killers had been convicted and put on death row.

Riley knew that Pennsylvania rarely actually executed criminals who were sentenced to death. Even so, it was obvious that these two murderers were safely behind bars and would be for the rest of their lives. So neither one of them could possibly be the killer she was looking for.

What she needed was an open case, a killer who had never been caught and was still at large. Or maybe a killer who had already served a sentence and was out on parole. But as hard as she searched, she couldn't find any such cases.

She took a long swallow of bourbon.

She felt herself sinking into despair now.

Why can't I crack this case? she wondered.

She'd been plagued by self-doubt ever since she'd arrived in Springett. She'd had a hard time getting any sense of this killer's psyche. Now she felt unsure of the ideas she had come up with. Was she wrong about this whole idea about family?

Were her unique abilities waning? Was her usefulness as an investigator coming to an end?

She remembered something that Blaine had said to her during their last conversation.

"Surely there are things you can do with the Bureau that don't involve such risk."

But were there, really?

Was she temperamentally suited to any other kind of work?

For that matter, was she temperamentally suited to anything else in life? Right now, she felt like a failure at everything she'd ever tried to do—a failure as a wife, lover, mother, and even simply a friend.

Somehow, she couldn't shake off the feeling that she'd even let Jenn down.

If she'd been a better partner, would Jenn have run away like that?

She took another swallow of bourbon, then murmured a single word aloud.

"Trust."

Just yesterday she'd been thinking that trust was in short supply for her these days. Blaine, Jilly, and April had all let her down, and now Jenn had let her down as well. But now she wondered—how could she expect to be able to depend on people when she herself kept falling short of their desires and needs?

Trust, after all, cut both ways.

Riley slumped in her chair. For a moment, she considered what Mike Nevins had said to her ...

"My door's always open, both figuratively and literally."

It had been a kind offer, and Riley knew that he had really meant it.

She wondered, *Should I knock on that door right now?*

She quickly decided not to. It was getting late, and Mike had already given her plenty of help for one day, and there would be time to talk with him about personal issues after this case was solved.

She took another swallow of bourbon and felt her last ounce of resolve ebbing away.

There's nothing else I can do, she thought.

At least not tonight.

Tomorrow she could begin afresh.

She poured another glass of bourbon, sat down on the bed propped up with pillows, and turned on the TV. She found a channel that was playing a movie she was pretty sure she'd seen before. But that didn't matter to her one way or the other. She didn't expect to pay much attention to it anyway. She was tired, and after another drink or two she'd surely go right to sleep.

As she stared at the images on the TV, her thoughts again wandered back to Jenn, and also to what Brent Meredith had said about finding her…

"I'll put our forensic technicians to work on that."

Riley scoffed and murmured, "Good luck with that, chief."

Riley knew enough about Jenn's skills and sheer cunning to be sure of one thing.

If Jenn didn't want to be found, she'd never be seen again.

CHAPTER TWENTY FOUR

The man stood looking out his apartment window, only half-hearing the TV in the next room. The news was on, and of course it was all about the murders. He felt no need for TV reporters to tell him what he already knew.

Instead he was staring at the apartment across the street. Its windows were dark and the young woman who lived there wasn't home yet. He wondered—was she going to come home tonight at all?

Such strange hours she keeps, he thought, with a touch of disapproval.

She came and went at the oddest times, and she almost always had friends coming and going with her. She was scarcely ever really alone.

Just like Rachel, he thought.

Indeed, he knew that her uncanny resemblance to his older sister in both appearance and behavior was much more than merely coincidental.

She is Rachel, after all.

She just didn't know it—and she wouldn't know it until a moment before her death, when he'd call her by that name.

He felt so lucky to have found her. But then, it surely wasn't just luck that had brought her into his life. Surely it was fate.

Just like the others, he thought.

He remembered the astonishing day when the first three had been revealed to him. It had happened so quickly. His purpose and duty had suddenly seemed so clear after so many years of struggling with guilt, grief, loneliness, and half-heard voices and shadowy ghosts flickering in and out of his hearing and sight.

He'd been walking past Wolfe's Furniture when he happened to glance through the front window and saw a dining room furniture set—a long table with six chairs. The style was exactly the same as the dining room furniture in his own childhood home. Those pieces of furniture could well have been the very table and chairs where his family had shared their meals, and where all of them were gathered on that fatal night.

All of them except me.

He remembered standing outside the furniture store staring raptly at the setting. Then he'd gone inside for a closer look and was even more astonished by the resemblance. The only real difference was that this furniture was new, and those back at home had shown the wear of years of happy use.

Still staring out his apartment window, he remembered wondering—did he dare sit down in the chair at his own place at the table? His heart had filled with joy at the idea. He couldn't resist. But as soon as he'd sat down, he'd been seized by a terrible sensation. A sense of accusation and chastisement had hung in the air.

When he'd stood up from the chair and turned around, he'd seen a familiar face.

Dad's face.

Their eyes had met and Dad's expression had seemed both sad and angry. Then Dad had turned away—and it seemed as if he wasn't Dad anymore. He was just a customer who'd come here with his nondescript wife to buy some furniture.

But then another pair of eyes met his, and these eyes were smiling and kindly. His heart had leapt with joy. There was no mistaking that face. It had been his sister Maureen.

Then Mo had turned her eyes away and didn't seem to be Mo anymore. Instead, she was a young female salesclerk handling a furniture sale to the man who looked so much like Dad.

He'd eavesdropped over the sale and caught their names. The man's name was Justin Selves, the girl's name was Drew Cadigan.

Or at least that's who they'd thought they were.

He'd wondered—how could he persuade them that they were wrong?

The man and his wife had bought some furniture and arranged for their delivery and left the store. He, too, had been on his way to the front door to leave when yet another pair of eyes met his.

Mom's eyes.

She'd been coming right inside, smiling at him. But their shared glance had lasted only for a fleeting instant, and she'd walked past him to talk to the salesclerk, acting like just another customer.

She, too, had made a purchase, and he had overheard her name—Joan Cornell.

After those confusing encounters he'd made his way home, his mind reeling from the strange way that fate was entering his life. Walking toward his apartment, he'd had no idea what to do next—not until a familiar young woman rode by him on her bicycle and smiled and waved at him, just as she seemed to do with everyone she met.

He'd almost collapsed right on the sidewalk there and then. Surely he must have seen this young woman a hundred times. She lived right across the street from him. And yet he'd never recognized her for who she really was.

My sister Rachel.

And at that moment, he'd known what had to be done. The three people he'd seen at the furniture store and this girl all had to die in order to be reborn as who they really were—Mom, Dad, Maureen, and Rachel.

And now, as he looked out the window, he saw three approaching bicycles glittering in streetlights.

She's back, he realized. *With two friends.*

As the girl and her friends got off their bicycles, he reached for his cell phone and snapped a picture of her. He didn't know whether he'd find a picture of her in her apartment when the time came, as he had with Mom and Dad and Maureen. But he already had several photos of her in his cell phone, and he'd choose one of them to frame and put on his table right here once everything had been taken care of.

Meanwhile, he watched and listened as she and the other two girls chattered and laughed as they parked their bikes and went inside the apartment building. Then the lights came on in the windows, and as he often could, he could see inside the little apartment that resembled his own.

She and her friends were darting around the kitchen area gathering up snacks from cabinets and the refrigerator. Then they put on some music and sat down to eat together at the little Formica-topped table with chairs made of chrome and yellow plastic padding.

He smiled a little at the thought of how odd one of those chairs would look alongside the others he'd collected so far. But he was sure Rachel would like it. It would suit her taste.

In fact, the girl seemed so much like Rachel right now. He remembered fondly how, before she'd moved away from home, she constantly had friends over, and laughter and music had poured out of her room.

Those times are coming back, Rachel, he thought.

Just you wait and see.

He turned away from the window and looked at the candlelit table, which took up so much space in his little apartment. As his eyes fell upon one empty space, his optimism was tainted by worry.

Where is Aunt Heather?

Like his sister Rachel, Aunt Heather was still absent. Her chair and portrait weren't there, and there was no hint of her shape or shadow. But he hadn't found her yet, and he certainly had no idea how he was going to bring her back into his life along with the rest of his family.

Patience, he told himself.

He had to keep faith that she'd reveal herself, just as all the others had. And when it happened, that moment too would feel like a magical moment of sheer destiny.

He walked into the room where the television was playing. The news as still on, and it was still about the deaths.

The news anchor was talking.

"The FBI is now involved in the investigation. One of the investigators to arrive here in the Philadelphia area is Special Agent Riley Paige. But she evaded reporters' questions this afternoon at the Springett police station..."

As the station played the footage from this afternoon, the man gasped at the sight of the woman who appeared on the TV screen.

"It's her!" he murmured aloud. "It's Aunt Heather!"

She was standing on the police station steps surrounded by reporters, looking harried and perplexed. And she kept saying...

"I've got no comment to make at this time."

The man felt a pang of pity for the woman who called herself Riley Paige.

He murmured aloud, "Of course you've got 'no comment.' You must feel terribly confused. You don't know who you are. You don't understand what's going on—and what's going to happen soon."

Then he touched the TV and added in a reassuring voice, "But don't worry. I'll take care of everything. Just leave it all up to me."

Of course he knew it wouldn't be easy. This woman was an FBI agent and not an easy target. But now that he thought about it, it made all the sense in the world that fate had saved his greatest challenge for last.

He smiled, feeling much better about the two killings that lay ahead. He couldn't change the past. But he could change the future. He could bring them all back. Soon they could sit and eat and laugh and talk together once again.

He turned off the TV and walked back to look at the dining room table. The shadowy ghosts were still silent, but he felt a thrill of happy anticipation hanging in the air.

Won't they be proud of me once I succeed? he thought.

CHAPTER TWENTY FIVE

Special Agent Bill Jeffreys felt a surge of conflicting emotions as he drove his rented car northward through the city of Philadelphia. None of those emotions were pleasant, and they were aggravated by the fact that he was very tired. The only thing good about having been rousted out of bed in the middle of the night was that the early morning traffic wasn't heavy. Having just arrived at the Philadelphia International Airport, he was headed to the well-to-do suburb of Springett.

Late last night, Bill had gotten a cryptic phone call from his boss, Brent Meredith. First Meredith had asked Bill how he was doing, and whether he felt ready to get back to work.

Bill had told him the truth—that he was feeling quite a bit better than he had a few days ago.

Then Meredith had gotten right to the point.

"Something has seriously gone wrong with Riley Paige's current assignment."

Bill had interrupted, *"Did something happen to Riley?"*

"No," Meredith had said. *"She's okay. But I need for you to go to Philadelphia and help her with the case she's working on."*

Bill had been startled. He'd thought Riley was working with their perfectly competent junior partner, Jenn Roston.

"Not anymore," Meredith had said. *"Roston has disappeared. Apparently she has resigned. That's why I need you to go work with Agent Paige."*

Bill had agreed right away to fly to Philadelphia, and Meredith arranged to have the FBI plane ready in the early morning hours. He'd left several phone messages for Riley, but had gotten no reply.

And now he was worried about her.

But he was also feeling somewhat pissed off. Taking some time off hadn't been his own idea, and he'd been annoyed ever since word got back to him that Riley and Jenn were working a case without him.

It was true that he'd been shaken by the outcome of the case the three of them had wrapped up just a couple of weeks ago. He'd had to use deadly force against a killer who almost killed Riley with an ice pick.

Nobody, including Bill, questioned that the shot had been fully justified. But using deadly force had never been easy for him, and this year it had gotten a lot harder than it used to be. When Meredith had put him on a short mandatory leave, Bill hadn't argued with him.

Still, to send his workmates out on a new case without even asking if he wanted to join them…

Bill growled under his breath as he neared the hotel where Riley was staying in Springett. He was mad at Meredith for not putting him on the Philadelphia case in the first place.

But he was also mad at himself.

I should have refused to take that leave, he thought.

Whatever had gone wrong between Riley and Jenn, surely he could have prevented it if only he'd been there.

Bill parked in front of a quaint little Colonial-style hotel called the Singer Inn. He ran his fingers through his slightly shaggy dark hair to smooth it out a bit, then went into the front lobby, identified himself to the desk clerk, and found out what room Riley Paige was staying in.

At the door of her room, Bill hesitated for a moment, wondering what to expect. Then he knocked and waited for an answer.

None came, and he knocked again.

This time he heard a groggy voice call out weakly, "Who is it?"

"It's Bill," he called. "Let me in."

He heard a gasp from inside the room. After a few seconds, Riley opened the door.

Bill was shocked by her appearance. Her face was pale and her eyes were red and her hair was a mess.

She actually seemed to be having trouble focusing her eyes on Bill.

"Jesus, Bill," she said in a hoarse voice. "What are you doing here?"

It's nice to see you too, Bill thought.

But he didn't say so aloud.

"Meredith sent me," he replied.

After a long, awkward moment, Riley stepped back and Bill came into the room.

"Why?" Riley asked.

"He didn't tell me exactly why, except that Jenn is gone."

With a sigh Riley said, "I guess he didn't tell you my FBI career is over."

Bill's mouth dropped open.

No, he didn't tell me that, he thought.

Glancing around the room, he could see that the covers on the bed were rumpled, but Riley hadn't slept under them, and she was fully clothed. He also noticed a near-empty bottle of bourbon on the nightstand.

Riley said with a slight laugh, "This is the part where I'm supposed to tell you this isn't as bad as it looks."

Bill nodded and said, "My guess is, it *is* as bad as it looks."

"Your guess is right," Riley said. With an exhausted sigh, she sat down on the end of the bed.

Bill sat down beside her, feeling at a loss for what to ask her next.

"I left you some voice mails," he said.

"I haven't been checking," Riley said.

Riley rubbed her forehead and added, "This is also the part where I'm supposed to break down crying in your arms and tell you how glad I am to see you. Believe me, I'd do that if I had the energy. I just feel too lousy right now."

Bill put his arm around her shoulder.

"Maybe later," he told her. "Right now you'd better get yourself cleaned up. It sounds like we've got work to do."

Riley nodded. She got to her feet a little unsteadily and headed straight to the bathroom. Soon Bill heard the shower start running. He sat there looking at the almost-empty bottle of bourbon.

She's had a really rough night, he thought.

He knew he ought to be angry with her for falling apart like this while working on a case. But how could he be angry?

I've been there, he thought.

He'd gone through his own personal hell during the weeks after he'd mistakenly shot an innocent man while working on a case in Southern California. The man hadn't been badly wounded, but Bill's error had stopped the wrong man, and that had probably cost a talented young agent her life.

His guilt over Lucy Vargas's death had been overwhelming. And the next time he'd needed to use deadly force, he'd frozen. He hadn't been able to do what he had to do.

He shook his head as he remembered how much bourbon he'd put away himself during that time, and also an awful text message he'd sent to Riley...

Just so you know. Been sitting here with a gun in my mouth.

It had been absolutely true, and Bill cringed at the memory.

Riley had gone AWOL from a case she and Jenn were working on to come to his rescue. He still didn't know how he could have gotten through that awful time without her friendship.

I can do the same for her, he thought.

Of course, it wouldn't be the first time for either of them. They'd pulled each other through many crises over the years.

After all, he thought—that's what partners were for.

Soon Riley emerged from the bathroom in clean clothes, still looking pretty haggard. She asked Bill what time it was.

When he told her, she said, "We're not too late for breakfast. Let's head on downstairs."

They went down to the dining area, where the hotel had set up a breakfast buffet. They picked up food and coffee, then found a table apart from the other guests.

Bill said to Riley, "This is the part where you tell me what the hell's going on."

Riley stared at her scrambled eggs for a moment.

Then she said, "Jenn's just gone."

"Gone where?" Bill asked.

"I don't know," Riley said. "But she's gone for good."

Riley let out a deep sigh and added, "The thing is, I knew she was gone first thing yesterday morning, but I spent a whole day covering for her. I should have called Meredith right away, but I kept hoping she'd come back, or at least know what she was doing. Then he called and told me she'd emailed him a letter of resignation."

"Why did she quit?" Bill asked.

"I don't know," Riley said. "She just left me a note saying 'sorry.' She didn't even explain herself in the letter to Meredith."

Bill could tell by Riley's voice that she wasn't telling him everything.

He leaned across the table toward her and said, "Riley, talk to me. Tell me what's going on."

Riley said in a voice choked with emotion, "I can't, Bill. I don't even know for sure."

Bill felt a flash of resentment. He'd long realized that Riley and Jenn had been sharing some secrets from him. He hadn't liked it. In all the years they'd worked together, neither he nor Riley had kept anything from each other, no matter how personal or painful or even humiliating. All that had changed when Jenn became part of their team. Bill had felt a certain distance between himself and Riley ever since.

After a long silence, Riley said, "There are things about Jenn that you don't know, Bill. You've got to trust me, it's best this way. I don't want you to be responsible for my own mistakes. Besides, it really doesn't matter anymore. She's gone for good."

Bill almost demanded that Riley tell him more.

But then he remembered how Jenn had covered for Riley when she'd gone AWOL to help him through his suicidal spell. It had been a risky and generous thing for Jenn to do, and Bill knew he and Riley both owed her for that.

And now he thought, *Riley seems ready to let Jenn go.*

He figured he mustn't question that.

"Meredith's furious with me," Riley said. "I don't blame him. He's got no reason ever to trust me again. I'm sure I'll have to resign unless he fires me first."

Although Bill didn't say so, he didn't think that was true. He hadn't detected any anger in Meredith's voice last night. Instead, Bill had strongly felt that Meredith was deeply worried about Riley. Maybe Riley hadn't noticed it, but Bill had long been aware that Meredith felt a deep paternal fondness for Riley.

Riley drew herself up and said, "Anyway, I've got one last case to solve. And I damn sure can't solve this one without a partner."

"Tell me all about it," Bill said.

He listened attentively as Riley explained everything.

CHAPTER TWENTY SIX

Riley's hangover and her despair both began to fade away. Telling Bill the details of the case was helping to clear her mind and lift her spirits. She couldn't help but feel that some kind of normality was restored now that her longtime partner was here. She thought his dark eyes looked tired, but—unlike Jenn during the last couple of days—Bill was his usual fully engaged self. He asked pertinent questions and made astute comments while keenly listening to Riley's every word.

Although she was still deeply disturbed by Jenn's abrupt disappearance, Riley was just now realizing how difficult their working relationship had become.

It felt good to be closely synced with Bill again. She had missed having this strong, quiet presence beside her.

Just like things are supposed to be, Riley thought.

It saddened Riley to think that her strange, secret-ridden relationship with her younger partner had put a certain distance between her and Bill.

But maybe we'll pull back together now.

Maybe things will soon be like they used to be.

As she ate breakfast and drank coffee, Riley told Bill everything that had happened since she had gotten here—the mistakes and dead-ends and false suspects, her impressions at the crime scenes and at Wolfe's Furniture, and her theory that the killer was trying to piece his lost family back together out of guilt for having murdered them.

Bill poked at his scrambled eggs with his fork and thought for a moment.

Then he said, "The question is, is he finished yet? How many family members did he kill in the first place?"

Riley nodded silently. It really was an important question, and a double-edged one as well. On one hand, it would obviously be good if he weren't tracking another victim right now, much less have killed someone already.

But on the other hand...

If he was finished with his twisted mission, if he'd succeeded to his own satisfaction, he'd be harder to apprehend and bring to justice. A dormant killer was always harder to catch than an active one.

They continued to eat in silence—a good kind of silence in which Riley knew they were productively processing their thoughts.

We're such a good team, she thought.

But they were more than that. They were best friends. Maybe, Riley thought, they were more than friends as well. Had she ever felt as close to Ryan or to Blaine as she felt to Bill? Had she ever shared her thoughts and feelings with those two men as openly and freely as she had with Bill?

No, she thought. *Not even close.*

She remembered something Brent Meredith had said over the phone.

"My own partners knew things about me that neither of my wives ever found out about."

Riley had heard other agents say much the same thing about their partners over the years. It was commonly understood among law enforcement officers that partners shared a peculiar kind of intimacy that didn't exist even in their marriages.

She thought, *Bill and I are just like any other partners, I guess.*

But then she wondered, was that really true? Was there something unique about her relationship with Bill?

Right now, looking across the table at him, she couldn't help but be aware of how attractive he was. He was craggier and a little less well-groomed than either Ryan or Blaine, but she liked him all the more for it.

She suppressed a shudder as she remembered another low moment in her life, nearly two years ago, when she'd tried to drown her misery in bourbon. She'd been freshly separated from her husband but Bill had still been married. In a near-stupor, she'd called and had made a pathetic drunken pass at him...

"I think about you, Bill. And not just at work. Don't you think about me, too?"

It had been an awful moment, and it had nearly ended their friendship.

Bill looked up at her and spoke, interrupting her thoughts.

"You told me you ran a computer search last night, right? Before you got drunk, I mean. I take it you couldn't find any pertinent cases of familicide in this area—aside from Leonard Robbins, I mean."

"That's not exactly true," Riley said. "I found two other cases. But they were both solved, and the killers are now on death row. There's no way either of them committed these recent killings."

Bill drummed his fingers on the table.

He said, "Riley, I've just got this weird feeling that we're looking at this from the wrong angle. Your theory's right, but we're approaching it the wrong way. I can't put my finger on what the problem is."

Riley nodded.

He's right, she thought. *I feel exactly the same way.*

They were close to the truth, perhaps even looking squarely at the truth, but still they somehow couldn't see it.

They both fell silent again. She thought back to her conversation with Mike Nevins, when her theory had really taken shape. She and Mike had agreed on an emotional profile that involved a "perfect storm" of loneliness and guilt.

Suddenly, she remembered something Mike had said to her—something even he'd admitted he didn't quite understand at the time...

"People don't always feel guilty over things they've done wrong. They can even feel guilty over things they were never really responsible for."

Riley felt a sudden tingling as her thoughts moved in a new direction.

She said, "Bill, I *have* been looking at this wrong. I've been assuming that our killer—well, that he'd always been a killer."

"Huh?" Bill said.

Riley leaned across the table toward him and said, "My key assumption is that he *lost* his family—that they're all dead and he's replicating those deaths for some twisted reason."

Bill's eyes widened as he seemed to understand what Riley was getting at.

"But he didn't necessarily *kill* his family," he said.

"No, and that's what's been hanging me up," Riley said.

"So are you suggesting that someone else murdered his family?" Bill asked.

Riley shook her head.

"I don't think so," she said. "I don't think vengefulness is driving him. My guess is that his whole family except for him died in some kind of accident. Maybe he had some reason to feel responsible for what happened, like it was his fault somehow."

Bill shrugged and said, "Or maybe he didn't have any reason to think so. He's obviously not rational, but if we're talking about survivor guilt, it doesn't have to be rational. Especially if the trauma happened when he was just a kid. He might have carried guilt around for years until he finally cracked..."

Riley and Bill sat staring at each other for a moment as these new ideas sunk in.

Finally Riley said, "My search was too limited last night. We've got to try it again."

They finished breakfast, then hurried back to Riley's room and sat down together at Riley's computer. They searched not for familicides but for incidents in which whole families had died in other ways. They found three instances of families dying in accidental ways, but at first they found none that fit what they were looking for.

Finally Bill said, "Here's something."

They both hastily read the newspaper article, which was dated twelve years ago. In the nearby suburb of Ongahela, a gas explosion blew up a whole house while the family that lived there was having dinner. A married couple, Joseph and Eva Crane, had been killed, along with their two daughters, Maureen and Rachel, and Joseph's sister, Heather Crane.

Riley said with a gasp, "But there was one survivor—Joseph and Eva's twelve-year-old son, Austin. He was outside playing when the explosion took place. He wasn't even injured."

"Talk about survivor guilt," Bill said. "Even if he's not our killer, that's one hell of a burden to carry around for the rest of one's life. If the kid's still alive, he's about twenty-four years old now."

Riley said, "And look at the ages. Joseph Crane was fifty-three at the time, and his wife was fifty-two. One of their daughters was nineteen. They were about the same age as Justin Selves, Joan Cornell, and Drew Cadigan."

Bill snapped his fingers and said, "That sure fits your theory. For some reason he's going after people that represent his lost family members."

Maybe, Riley thought.

But she warned herself not to get her hopes up. There were still a lot of unanswered questions and the last thing she wanted to do right now was to jump to any wrong conclusions.

She said to Bill, "If we're right, two of his family members still aren't represented by victims—a twenty-four-year-old older sister, and an aunt who was in her forties when she died. That would mean he's not finished yet."

Shore took the call, which Riley put on speakerphone. She explained that she was working with a different partner, Bill Jeffreys, who was participating in the call.

Shore said, "I figured I'd be hearing from you pretty soon, Agent Paige. Robbins made a confession right after you left, but only to killing his family. I leaned on him hard, but that was all I got. And the truth is, I now think you were right. He didn't commit the three recent murders."

He let out an embarrassed cough and added, "Anyway, you've now got my full attention."

"Okay," Riley said, feeling relieved, "Here's what I need to do now. Do you happen to remember a gas explosion that took place over in Ongahela twelve years ago? A whole family was killed, and—"

Shore interrupted, "Oh, yeah, I remember that. An awful business. Just one kid survived, a twelve-year-old. If I remember right, he wound up in the foster system after it happened."

Bill put in, "His name was Austin Crane. We'd like to know what happened to him in the years after that."

Riley heard Shore gasp.

"Are you thinking he might be a suspect?" he asked.

Bill said, "Maybe. It's something we need to check out right away."

Shore said, "Well, if he's still in the area, I ought to be able to track him down."

Riley heard Shore's fingers clacking away on a keyboard for a few moments.

Then he said in an excited voice, "I've found him. He lives right here in Springett."

"What can you tell us about him?" Bill asked.

"Not much from the information I've got here," Shore said. "But it looks like he works at home doing data entry."

Bill nodded and said, "So he's maybe a loner. That might fit."

Shore said, "So what do you want us to do? Go over to where he lives, pay him a visit, and have a little talk with him?"

Riley scratched her chin and said, "I don't know. I'd like to have a little more leverage than that."

Shore scoffed and said, "Well, it doesn't sound like we've got enough on him to get an arrest warrant for him."

Bill said, "Maybe not. But maybe we can get a search warrant."

"How do you figure?" Shore said.

Riley said, "My partner's right. He and I are both trained profilers, and yesterday I spoke with a forensic psychiatrist to develop some theories. Based on our combined expertise, Austin Crane sounds like a person of interest, at the very least."

Bill added, "And we've got specific items to search for—three stolen chairs and three stolen pictures."

Shore agreed. "That might well be enough to go on. I'll contact Judge Knight right away and see what he can do. Meanwhile, I'll give you Crane's address. Let's meet there ASAP. If we're lucky, I'll have a search warrant with me. Otherwise … well, we'll just play it by ear."

They ended the call, and Bill looked at Riley with a surprised expression.

He said, "Do you think Shore can get a warrant that fast?"

Riley chuckled a little and said, "Based on what happened yesterday, Chief Shore and Judge Knight are pretty cozy together, and they both like to get things done in a hurry. I wouldn't be surprised."

"Well, let's get going then," Bill said.

He and Riley headed out of the hotel to his rented car.

As Bill started to drive, Riley wondered …

Are we closing in on the killer?

She wanted to think so.

But she knew that a search for a monster seldom turned out to be that simple.

CHAPTER TWENTY SEVEN

Riley felt her anticipation rising as Bill drove them into the neighborhood where Austin Crane lived. The area they entered seemed peaceful—almost disarmingly so. But Riley knew better than to be lulled by appearances. In her experience, tranquil places like this sometimes harbored the most terrible twisted psyches.

It was a well-worn neighborhood, with sturdy old trees and streets lined with grass along the curbs. Wide stairways led from the sidewalks up to spacious porches, and many of the three-story brick buildings featured bay windows.

Riley figured that these places were built in the 1920s or '30s. Back then, the neighborhood must have been considered rather upscale. Judging from the variety of pedestrians Riley saw, people of more modest means lived here these days. But she could see that they weren't poor. And the way they smiled and waved and greeted one another told Riley that this was a pleasant place where people knew and trusted each other, the kind of neighborhood that was fast vanishing in these days of gentrification.

They arrived at the address Chief Shore had given them, and Bill parked in front of the building where Austin Crane lived.

Bill asked Riley, "What do you want to do now?"

"Wait for Chief Shore," Riley said.

Bill chuckled a bit and said, "Sounds like a plan."

As they sat in the car, Riley again felt as if some kind of normalcy had returned to her life now that she was working with Bill again. The very silence between them felt easy and natural—and at the same time, she knew they were both mentally preparing for what might happen next. They were trying to trap a monster.

She and Bill had been through this together hundreds of times before. And she knew perfectly well that just about anything could happen. If Austin Crane really was the killer, what should they expect to happen when they confronted him?

She didn't yet have any feeling as to whether this killer was particularly cunning or intelligent. Would he be fully prepared for their search, having hidden any physical evidence where they couldn't possibly find it? Would he be a smooth talker with well-developed alibis to cover for his whereabouts during the times of the murders?

Or would he be foolish and incompetent and easy to bring to justice?

Or...

Riley didn't want to think about another possibility, which was that they'd tracked down the wrong man altogether. The last thing she wanted to face right now was another dead end.

Soon Chief Shore arrived in an unmarked van and parked in the space in front of their car. While the chief himself was dressed in civilian clothes, Riley was dismayed to see that he'd brought along two uniformed cops.

She let out a discouraged groan.

Obviously taken aback as well, Bill muttered, "Uh-oh. I don't like the looks of that."

Riley said, "I guess I should have told him to come with plain-clothes guys."

"Well, you can't think of everything," Bill said.

Riley glanced up at the building windows, looking for a face that might be peering down at them. But the windows were too dark for her to see anything like that.

She and Bill had been counting on the element of surprise. What would the suspect do if he saw in advance that cops were headed for his apartment right now? Would that be all the notice he needed to prepare himself for their arrival?

Riley said, "We'd better get in there quickly."

Bill nodded in agreement.

As they got out of the car, Chief Shore and his cops came walking toward them. Shore waved a search warrant at Riley and Bill.

"We're ready to go," he said.

Without another word, they all walked up the building's front steps and across its front porch. Riley was relieved that the front door opened without them having to be buzzed inside.

In the front hallway, Riley could see that the building had once been a single residence. It had been broken down into apartments that were accessed by a central staircase. The whole place was silent as they climbed two flights.

There were two apartments on the top floor. Riley knocked sharply on the door where the suspect lived.

No one answered, and she knocked again.

Bill called out, "Austin Crane, this is the FBI. We need to talk to you."

Again there was no answer.

Riley was really worried now.

She said to Chief Shore, "I need for one of your guys to go check and see if there's a back exit out of this building. Or a fire escape on the back. If he sneaked out that way, he probably hasn't gotten very far."

Chief Shore nodded at one of his cops, who headed down the stairs.

But the other cop clearly had different ideas. He was trying the doorknob.

In a warning voice, Shore said to him, "I wouldn't do that, Ornstein. We don't have a no-knock warrant. We can't just—"

But before he could finish his sentence, the cop named Ornstein slammed his body against the door, which flew wide open.

Looking quite pleased with himself, Ornstein stepped back into the hallway and said, "Lookit that. It just opened by itself. The deadbolts in these old buildings aren't worth shit. Let's go in there and have a look around."

Chief Shore's face reddened with anger.

"Goddamn it, Ornstein," he said. "You know better than to pull that kind of crap."

But now that the door stood open, Riley stood transfixed by what she saw just inside, and she instinctively drew her weapon.

She was looking into a long room, obviously the main room of that apartment. It was crowded by a dining room table that was too large for the space it occupied. Chairs were placed at each end, and two others along one side.

Riley immediately recognized three of those chairs. Two were nicely designed and looked new. The third was similar but well-worn.

They had all been stolen from murder scenes.

"Good Lord," Chief Shore murmured.

There could be no question about it.

They had found the home of the killer.

There no longer seemed much point in following protocol. Riley walked inside the apartment, and the others followed.

At that moment, the cop who had been sent downstairs returned.

He said, "There's a back exit down on the first floor, but it's still bolted from the inside. There's an old fire escape that looks like it hasn't been used in years. No one has gone out that way recently."

Chief Shore ordered the other two cops to search the apartment to make sure Austin Crane wasn't hiding here someplace. Riley holstered her weapon again. Although she felt sure they wouldn't find him here in his apartment, she didn't know whether to feel relieved or not. Perhaps the killer had left here a while ago and had no idea of their arrival. But did that give them any advantage?

Maybe, she thought.

Perhaps they could station themselves here or return to their vehicles and lie in wait for him. But hadn't they already made themselves too conspicuous to conduct an effective stakeout? If he did know they were there, would he even return here at all?

Riley really wished Ornstein hadn't smashed that door open. If he hadn't, they might be seated in their vehicles watching out for him right this minute. When he returned, they could have confronted him and conducted a legitimate search, which would have revealed what they now saw. They could have arrested him on the spot.

But things were playing out very differently.

And where might Austin Crane be right now?

Riley felt a deep chill at the thought that he might be claiming his next victim at this very moment.

"We've got to find him," she said to the others. "Chief Shore, did your initial search for him bring up any photos of him?"

Shore nodded and said, "I got his driver's license photo."

Riley said, "We need to make that image public, get the media involved. Put out an APB on him. Let's make sure that anyone who sees him reports him right away."

"I'll get right on it," Shore said.

He stepped out into the hall to call in instructions on his cell phone. Meanwhile, Riley stood looking at the table.

Sure enough, there were three framed pictures on the table where the stolen chairs were placed—one of Justin Selves, another of Joan Cornell, and another of Drew Cadigan. There were lots of unlit candles on the tabletop and the surrounding furniture.

She heard Bill say, "Riley, have a look at this."

She turned and saw him looking at a large framed picture that hung prominently on the wall near the table. It was a family portrait that showed a mother, a father, two teenage girls, a boy of about twelve, and a woman who appeared to be close to the parents' age.

"They're all here—all the people who died in that explosion," Bill said. "Joseph and Eva Crane, their daughters, Maureen and Rachel, and Joseph's sister, Heather. Plus the kid who wasn't there at the time. The whole room is like a shrine."

Riley felt a shudder of agreement.

What was more, the mother and father and the younger sister strongly resembled the three people who had been murdered so far.

Riley said, "He's hunting for lookalikes—doppelgangers, almost."

"Yeah, and check this out," Bill said, pointing to one of the faces.

Looking at the woman who was apparently Heather Crane, Riley immediately saw what Bill meant. The woman looked jarringly like Riley herself. The coincidental resemblance felt truly weird to Riley.

She guessed that Austin had already picked out another lookalike for his aunt by now. Whoever it was had no idea of the danger she was in—nor did whoever he'd found who looked like his sister Rachel.

Riley wished she could reach out to both women and warn them.

As she looked around, she found it easy to imagine how the room would look bathed in candlelight. She also found it easy to imagine Austin's twisted mental state as he gazed upon this scene.

She took a few deep breaths, trying again to get a better sense of him.

"Are you getting anything?" Bill whispered.

Riley didn't reply immediately. But she remembered something she'd said to Mike Nevins yesterday...

"He's a collector, Mike. He collects chairs and portraits, but his obsession goes much deeper than that."

Riley said to Bill, "He collects things. He's trying to collect..."

Her voice faded away as she tried to put her feeling into words.

Bill said, "Yeah, I can see he's collecting chairs and photos. But what good does he think this collection is going to do for him?"

"He's trying to collect his family back," Riley said.

Bill scoffed slightly.

"By stealing tables and chairs?" he said. "And why is he killing his family's lookalikes? What does that have to do with anything?"

Riley felt a mounting tingle of realization. She couldn't yet put her finger on what it was.

"He's confused, Bill," she said. "Part of him thinks that the people he kills *are* his family members."

"So why does he kill them?" Bill said. "Isn't that like making them die all over again? It doesn't make sense to me."

Riley gasped as the truth came into focus.

She said, "Think about it, Bill. By killing them ... he's actually..."

Her voice faded, but she saw a similar growing realization in Bill's eyes.

"My God," Bill said. "He's collecting their—"

Bill was interrupted as Ornstein stepped out from the next room.

"This room is his office, where he does his data work," Ornstein said. "I've tried to get into his computer, but I can't do it without his password. I guess we'll have to turn it over to our tech guys to figure it out."

Riley and Bill stared at each other for a silent moment.

Then Riley said to Ornstein, "Try 'soul.'"

With a look of mild surprise, Ornstein went back into the next room.

A few seconds later he called out…

"It works."

Riley felt weak in the knees and had to sit down.

The whole thing made terrifying sense now. The killings themselves were ritualistic, meant to reclaim the souls of his lost family members.

And once he's got all those souls…

Austin Crane fully expected to resurrect them all—to literally bring them back from the dead.

She hadn't grasped the depth of his insanity until just this moment.

Nor had she realized how horribly dangerous he was.

CHAPTER TWENTY EIGHT

Austin Crane ran. He ran blindly, mindlessly, like some small animal pursued by a beast of prey. He felt as though the cool morning air was scorching his lungs.

Finally Austin simply couldn't run anymore. He slowed to a halt and looked around, gasping for breath. He saw that he'd run all the way to the Turner Meade supermarket, in Springett's old outdoor shopping mall. He collapsed panting onto a bench at the edge of the parking lot, sweating and gasping.

What just happened? he wondered.

The morning had started out so well. Off and on all night, he'd been checking the young woman's apartment across the street. Through her big bay windows, he could see them watching TV and laughing and talking. This morning he hadn't been able to see into her window, but after a while he'd seen her two friends leave and ride away on their bicycles.

He knew she would be alone now. Even better, today was Saturday, and she wouldn't be hurrying off to work. His opportunity had arrived at last. Soon, very soon, he'd call the woman by her real name...

Rachel.

He'd picked up his knife and slipped it into a crude ankle sheath he'd made out of an old tennis shoe. Then he'd left his apartment and headed across the street to the building where she lived. He'd been standing on the big front porch, gathering up his resolve to enter the building, when he heard a car pull to a stop across the street.

He'd stepped back into the shadows of the porch and watched as the driver parked a van in front of his own building. He'd felt a brief tingle of alarm when three men got out, because two of them were wearing police uniforms.

He told himself that they surely hadn't come here on his account.

But then the men were joined by two other people who arrived in another car—a man and a woman.

He'd shivered deeply when he'd immediately recognized the woman's face.

Aunt Heather.

He couldn't have mistaken anyone else for her. Then he'd remembered seeing her on the news last night—Special Agent Riley Paige, the news anchor had called her.

His panic had exploded inside him as the people he was watching went into his own apartment building.

Without stopping to think, he'd left the porch and broken into a run.

And he'd kept running until he'd gotten here just now.

Now that he had time to think about what he'd done, he was furious with himself.

I shouldn't have run, he thought.

I should have gone right ahead and done what I meant to do.

It had still been the perfect time, with the young woman alone in her apartment. The FBI woman and the cops need not have known what he was doing.

I could have done it, he thought.

By now, I could have told Rachel who she was.

He could have watched with awed wonder as her soul poured out of her body.

But he'd failed to do it. Worse still, he'd also failed to realize how fate had brought the FBI woman right to his front door—the woman who didn't yet know she was Aunt Heather. It was hard to imagine how he could have killed her too. But surely fate would have offered him a way—if only he hadn't panicked and run.

And now, sitting here on this bench, he almost wept with shame and bitterness.

Had he ruined everything?

Had he spoiled his final chance to complete his life's sole great purpose?

In the morning breeze, he thought he heard Mom's voice echoing through the air...

"Austin! Dinner's ready!"

He shuddered as the whole awful incident came back to him. His family had been looking forward to an especially nice dinner together. Even Aunt Heather had joined them. But when Mom had called him in from outside, he hadn't felt ready to stop playing. He'd ignored her repeated calls.

Finally he'd heard her yell crossly, *"All right, then. We're going to go ahead and eat without you."*

About a minute later, an explosion had thrown him off his feet. When he'd picked himself up, he'd seen his own home disintegrating in a huge ball of flame.

And now he could swear that he heard Mom's voice again calling...

"Austin! Dinner's ready!"

He fought down a sob of guilt and shame. During all the years since the explosion, he'd wondered—if he'd simply answered her call and gone to dinner, would the gas explosion never have happened? Was it fate's way of punishing him for his childish behavior? Or had fate meant him to die along with them?

He gritted his teeth and thought...

I've got to answer that call at long last.

I can't let them down.

The three souls he'd already gathered deserved to see his task completed.

He breathed slowly and deeply. It was time to gather his wits and renew his resolve. Now that he could think more clearly, he considered the fact that the police had just gone to his apartment. He wondered, what had they done there?

Had they gone inside?

Had they found his shrine?

One thing seemed clear. They were now after *him*. And if he hoped to complete his mission, he had to do it without getting caught. And that meant having some idea of what the cops and the FBI were up to.

He'd been following the news about the murders on TV. So far, he'd seen nothing to alarm him. But now, of course, things had changed. How much danger was he really in?

He took out his cell phone and brought up his news feed.

Almost immediately, he saw his own photo with his name and a detailed description of him—and a warning that he was dangerous.

He gasped aloud as he realized...

There's an APB out for me.

His thoughts were in chaos as he struggled to think what to do.

As he gazed wildly around the shopping area, an answer began to form in his mind.

❧ ❧ ❧

Things were moving much faster than Riley had believed possible. With Bill driving his rented car, they were following closely behind Chief Shore's van as he tracked the killer.

Bill said, "I sure hope this stingray gambit doesn't backfire on us. Legally, I mean."

Riley thought about it for a moment, then replied, "As I understand the law, stingray results can't be used as primary evidence. We're not going to be using it that way. We're just trying to locate the killer. It should be OK."

"I hope you're right," Bill said.

Riley had been only mildly surprised to learn that Shore had a stingray device in his van—an electronic tool for tracking the positions of cell phones. She knew stingrays were becoming more and more common among local police departments, even if their use still occupied a gray legal area. Police officials who used them had to sign a nondisclosure agreement promising the FBI never to admit that the department even had such a device.

She felt growing approval of the police chief. He seemed to be a wily sort who liked to push the limits of legality. Right now that seemed to her like a good thing.

Along with Austin Crane's driver's license photo, Chief Shore already had also found his cell phone number. That was all the chief had needed to put the stingray to work. Riley had been startled at how easily the stingray had picked up a "ping" showing Crane's actual location.

She and Bill were following Shore to that location right now.

She wondered what the killer was doing. Did he have any idea that they'd been to his apartment? There was no particular reason to think so. He might not even know that he was considered a suspect. Perhaps he was just out socializing or doing errands. She wished she had some idea of his current mental state.

They followed the police van into the wide parking lot of an older shopping area. The van parked near a large supermarket, and Bill pulled to a stop right next to it.

By the time they got out of their car, Shore was pacing like a cage animal, alternately surveying the area and looking at an electronic pad in his hand.

"Where the hell is the bastard?" the chief snarled. "The ping is coming from right here. He's got to be here somewhere. But where is he?"

Riley turned slowly around, looking for some sign of the man they were looking for. Then her eyes fell on something that made her spirits sink. At the edge of the parking lot, to one side of the supermarket, was an enormous metal dumpster.

Shore had just focused on that too. Following the tracking on his electronic pad, he strode toward the dumpster.

"You've got to be kidding me," he growled.

Riley nodded ruefully.

"He knows we're after him," she said. "He threw his cell phone in the dumpster. God knows where he is by now."

Shore sat down on a nearby bench and hunched over miserably. "So what do we do now?" he asked.

Riley and Bill looked at each other. Bill nodded, and Riley knew they were both thinking the same thing. She also knew that Shore and his men weren't going to like hearing it.

Bill said to Shore, "We've got to get that phone, and we can't wait for the garbage truck. You were able to track that phone, so it's still functional. It might have important information on it."

Shore waved his arms in protest.

"No, no, no," he said. "We already looked at his computer back in his apartment. We didn't find anything there except work and games and innocent-looking emails, most of them having to do with business."

"We can't be sure it will be the same with the phone," Riley said. "We've got to find out."

Shore shrugged his shoulders wearily and said to the cop named Ornstein, "You heard what the lady said. Search the goddamn dumpster."

Growling with dismay, Ornstein pointed to his partner.

"Why me?" he said. "Why can't Packwood here do it?"

Shore snapped at him, "Consider it your punishment for busting through the door back at Crane's apartment. The way I see it, you're getting off easy, at least if that's the worst thing that happens to you."

The cop named Packwood stood gloating as Ornstein lifted the dumpster lid and climbed inside.

A few seconds later Ornstein called out, "I've got it."

His uniform stained and strewn with garbage, Ornstein climbed out of the dumpster and handed the smelly phone to Riley. As Bill and Shore watched over her shoulders, she clicked the phone on and immediately got the command, ENTER PASSCODE.

Without hesitating, she typed in "SOUL."

Sure enough, the phone opened for her.

As Shore watched, he muttered, "Nicely done."

Riley looked over the icons and found where Crane kept his cell phone photos. Sure enough, when she clicked into them she saw a group of photos that made chills run through her body.

Some of the shots were not very clear, but she knew they were of people who were dead now. The images of the man and the woman seemed to have been taken as they looked at furniture. Others were of a young girl who seemed to be working there. Wolfe's furniture had been part of this this nightmare after all—just not the way Riley had first thought.

Then she found a series of photos of a young woman who looked remarkably like Rachel Crane in the family portrait. Those seemed to have been taken surreptitiously in various locations. The young woman surely had no idea that Crane had snapped them—or even that he'd taken any notice of her.

"That's his next intended victim," Riley said to Bill and Shore.

"We can't let that happen," Shore said. "But he's still at large, and my guess is he's more dangerous than ever. We've got to find this girl. Agent Jeffreys, could you get your FBI technicians to do some kind of facial recognition search?"

Bill said, "Maybe, but it will take time."

Shore said with a sigh, "Time is something we probably don't have much of. But we've got nothing else to go on."

As Riley kept skimming the photos, she noticed a few especially creepy ones. They appeared to have been taken at night from outside looking in through the woman's big bay windows.

They hadn't been taken from below, but from straight on.

The man taking the photo had been at the same level as the woman he was watching.

With a jolt of realization, she spoke to her colleagues.

"Never mind facial recognition. I know where she lives."

CHAPTER TWENTY NINE

For a moment, Austin Crane was disconcerted by the reflection. The silver glass tiles covering one of the hotel lobby walls were almost like a mirror, but he felt as though he was looking at a stranger.

After the small shock faded, he was very pleased.

An excellent disguise, he thought.

Austin was proud of how clear-headed he'd become after that spell of panic when he'd thrown his cell phone into the dumpster back at the mall. He'd pulled himself together and walked boldly over to one of the smaller stores, fully aware that he might be recognized on account of the APB with his picture. But he'd had to take that risk.

Fortunately, he'd had plenty of cash in his wallet. He'd gone into a thrift shop where he'd bought a wig, a purse, makeup, and women's clothes—a high-necked pink blouse with businesslike gray slacks and a blazer.

Then he'd ducked into a public restroom and put on his disguise.

And now, looking again at himself in the mirror-like wall, he was more than satisfied with the results. He'd done a good job with the makeup, keeping it subtle. He also realized that he was lucky to have found a good wig that didn't look at all fake. He certainly wasn't likely to be recognized, especially not with these bangs that obscured the basic shape of his face.

Smoothing back the long black hair with one hand, Austin smiled as he realized, *I'm actually rather pretty.*

He remembered how his sisters had always envied his soft complexion and long, graceful eyelashes. Then he almost turned away from his reflection for fear that people might notice him admiring himself.

But then he thought, *Why should I worry about that?*

He'd seen women pausing to check their appearances in mirrors and reflective surfaces all the time. But he figured it probably wasn't a good idea to overdo it. Besides, he had other much more important things to concern himself with right now.

Austin sat down on a plush sofa in the lobby and opened up a complimentary newspaper. While pretending to read, he kept an eye on the man and woman he'd followed here. He was feeling confident and hopeful. After all, his audacious acts had gotten him this far very successfully.

After disguising himself, he'd hurried on foot back to the street where he lived, planning to do exactly what he'd meant to do earlier. He would knock on the young woman's door, get himself invited into her apartment, and call her by Rachel's name and claim her soul once and for all. Then he'd find some way to reach his last victim, taking Aunt Heather's soul as well.

But when he'd approached the apartment building, the first thing he'd seen was that woman—the FBI agent who didn't yet know that she was Aunt Heather, the one people called Riley Paige. She'd been coming out of the building with the man who'd been with her earlier. And between them had been the girl herself, looking dazed and frightened.

He'd been stunned to realize—the police had somehow found out who his next target was supposed to be. And now they were taking her away.

But he hadn't given in to panic, not that time.

He saw that fate had dealt him a startling opportunity.

Right at that moment, a taxi had been dropping off one of Austin's neighbors at a nearby building. When the FBI agents had started driving away with the young woman, he'd rushed to catch the taxi, saying to the driver...

"Oh, dear—my friends just drove off without me. Could you follow them, please?"

He'd spoken in a soft, sweet voice, and he'd noticed the taxi driver smiling back flirtatiously in his mirror as he drove. The taxi had followed the car right here to the hotel, and the two FBI agents had rushed the young woman inside while Austin had been paying the driver.

By the time Austin got into the lobby, the FBI woman and her partner were there, but he saw no sign of the young woman they were protecting. He was sure somebody else must have already rushed her to a room for safekeeping.

Now all he could do was keep his eye on the FBI woman and her partner. They were standing across the lobby talking with a man he guessed to be some kind of plainclothes officer.

Finally the FBI woman and her partner finished their conversation with the other man. As they walked in Austin's direction, he overheard the partner say to the woman, "You go on up to the room. I'm going to the car to get my go-bag, then I'll check myself in."

The woman nodded and headed straight toward the elevator while her partner continued on his way outside.

Austin got up from the sofa and hurried along behind her. When she and a couple of other people stepped into the elevator, he did too. Making himself inconspicuous, he stood with a man between himself and the woman. Not noticing Austin at all, the woman pushed the button for the third floor.

As the elevator rose, Austin realized—the FBI woman might well be on her way to the room where the girl was being kept. All Austin had to do now was follow her to find out where that was.

When the elevator stopped at the third floor, he got off with the woman, taking care to walk some distance in the opposite direction down the hall. He ducked into a recessed area that held an ice machine and a couple of vending machines. Then he peeked around the corner and saw the woman he had followed talking to a man who stood stiffly at one of the hotel room doors.

Austin couldn't hear what they were saying from that distance, but the situation seemed perfectly clear. The man was an armed guard posted to protect the young woman he was trying to find.

When they finished talking, the FBI woman walked over to a neighboring door and went inside that room.

Austin almost gasped aloud at how splendidly things were unfolding.

Rachel and Aunt Heather!

In rooms right next to each other!

Soon, he'd gain access to both of them.

Soon, his task would be finished.

Of course he knew it wouldn't end as perfectly as he'd once hoped, with the whole family sitting around the dining room table with their own portraits bathed in candlelight. Now that the police had invaded his apartment, that was no longer possible.

But now that he thought about it, maybe it was better this way. He would have secured the souls he needed. Once that was done, he could hold exactly that scene in his mind, carry it around inside him wherever he went for the rest of his life.

It will be truly perfect after all, he thought.

Meanwhile, as his brain began hatching a plan, he knew there was an obstacle he needed to overcome.

The guard, he thought. *I've got to get him out of the way.*

And he knew exactly what he was going to have to do to make that happen.

And yet he wondered ...

Do I dare?

He breathed deep and long and felt his resolve building inside him. Yes, he could do this. He had no choice but to do it. It was either that or abandon his purpose altogether. He'd come much too far to give up now.

Besides, he could feel fate beckoning to him, showing him the way.

In the recessed area next to the machines was a door marked EMPLOYEES ONLY. He tried the doorknob and found that the door was unlocked and led into a small room that held supplies and cleaning equipment.

Perfect, he thought.

He took a compact out of his purse. Studying his appearance, he removed a hairclip from his wig so that the hair fell more freely on his shoulders. Then he took a deep breath and stepped out into the hallway. He called out to the guard in the same feminine voice he had used with the cab driver.

"Excuse me, sir."

The man turned and looked.

With slight giggle and a calculated note of shyness in his voice, Austin spoke again.

"I'm sorry to trouble you, but this vending machine is stuck. I keep putting money into it, but nothing comes out. It's such a nuisance, and I don't know what to do. I just wondered … could you help me with it?"

The guard smiled in a way that reminded Austin of the cab driver's smile in the mirror.

"I'd be glad to," he said.

The guard walked down the hall and stepped into the recessed area. He grinned at Austin and then peered at the machines.

"Now which one is giving you so much trouble?" he asked.

Behind the guard's back, Austin had already drawn the knife from his purse.

With one swift motion, he slit the man's throat.

The guard's eyes bulged as he made choking noises and fell to the floor, writhing in agony. Austin opened the employees' door and wrestled the still-writhing guard into the supply room. He watched while the guard began to fade into unconsciousness, his eyes still wide open.

Then Austin bent forward and unpinned the dying man's badge from his shirt, taking note of his name. He took the man's handkerchief out of his jacket pocket and wiped the blood off his knife and also his hands.

Then he stepped out of the supply room and shut the door, leaning against it and breathing hard for a moment. He looked around and saw that some blood had spurted onto one of the vending machines and onto the floor. But he'd moved the body quickly and there wasn't as much bloodstain as he might have expected. Certainly no one would notice it from the hallway. By the time someone saw the stains, they would have no reason to connect the blood with him.

As he hurried away, Austin felt an almost uncontrollable surge of wild exaltation.

I did it! he thought.

He'd had no idea that he was capable of killing anyone not directly linked to his mission.

He steadied himself again and continued along the hall to the doors where the two women were staying.

He chose one of the doors and knocked.

CHAPTER THIRTY

Joyce Rowland jumped to her feet at the sound of the knock at the door. She'd just stretched out on the hotel bed trying to calm herself down, but now she was standing again, shaking all over.

A fight or flight response, she realized.

It was hardly any surprise, considering how her whole world had suddenly been turned so horribly upside down. It seemed like only a minute ago when those FBI agents had arrived at her apartment to tell her that her life was in danger. They'd whisked her away to this hotel in an incredible hurry.

She still couldn't get it through her head that all this was really happening.

There was another knock, and a voice gently calling out, "Are you all right?"

Joyce walked over to the door and looked out through the peephole. She saw a smiling woman's face and an FBI badge.

The woman said through the door, "I'm just checking in with you. I hope that's all right."

Joyce breathed easier.

Another FBI agent, she thought. *The more the merrier.*

She'd be glad to have a whole army protecting her from that killer.

She opened the door, and the young woman came inside, still smiling. In her businesslike attire, she looked more like Joyce's image of a female FBI agent than the woman who had helped bring her here—Riley Paige was her name—who'd been more casually dressed.

Tucking the badge inside her blazer, the woman gently shook Joyce's hand.

She said, "I'm Agent Tina Hadley, from the Philadelphia FBI field office. I believe you've already met Eric Barnes."

Joyce nodded. Agent Barnes was the man who had been posted outside her door.

Tina Hadley said, "Well, I'll be sharing Agent Barnes's watch. He went down to the cafe to get us some coffee. I thought I'd take a minute to come inside and introduce myself."

"That's very kind of you," Joyce said.

She meant that sincerely. All the agents who had dealt with her with so far, including Agent Barnes, had been brusque and efficient. It wasn't that they'd seemed deliberately unfriendly. But they'd clearly had a job to do and didn't want to waste time about it.

They'd alerted Joyce to the basic facts of her situation—that a man who lived across the street from her planned to kill her, as he had three other people recently. They'd shown her his picture and told her his name and asked whether she knew him personally. She did not, although she recognized his picture. She remembered waving and saying hi to him once in a while when they were both out walking. Otherwise, she'd barely ever noticed him.

Joyce said to Tina, "Please sit down."

Agent Hadley let out a reluctant little laugh and said, "OK, but only for just a minute."

Joyce led the agent to the sitting area, and they both took seats at the table.

Tilting her head sympathetically, Tina asked, "Tell me—how are you holding up?"

Joyce sighed deeply. It was truly a relief to be asked that simple question at long last.

She said, "Oh, Agent Hadley—"

"Call me Tina, please," the agent said.

"OK, Tina. I feel like I'm ... well, I almost feel like I must be losing my mind. I can't believe this is happening. I saw stories on the news about this killer, but I never imagined … Do you have any idea why that man would want to kill me?"

Tina shrugged slightly.

"We're working on a theory," Tina said. "But … well, sometimes it's very hard to explain why people do certain things. It's human nature, I guess."

"I suppose it is," Joyce agreed.

"But I promise you, you're safe now," Tina said. "Everybody on our team has done this before. We've never lost anybody. We'll protect you."

Joyce's mood darkened a little over that phrase …

"We've never lost anybody."

It was disturbing to be reminded of the possible consequences of failure.

Tina's smile broadened and she said, "Everything's going to be just fine, Rachel."

Joyce felt a jolt of perplexity.

She said, "My name's … not …"

Tina's eyes narrowed in a curious expression.

"Not Rachel?" she said. "Oh, I'm sure it is."

Joyce was beginning to feel uneasy. Why would a trained FBI agent make a mistake like this? It seemed very odd to her.

She said, "No, really, my name's not Rachel. Surely you know … my name is …"

Her voice faded.

She wondered, *Why should I have to tell her what my name is?*

Tina chuckled and said, "What? Your name is what?"

Joyce shivered deeply with confusion.

Doesn't she think I know my own name? she wondered.

Something was very wrong here. Joyce felt sure of it.

Her voice cracking in a peculiar way now, Tina said, "You don't recognize me, do you?"

Joyce sputtered, "I … we just met and …"

Joyce's voice trailed off again. This was beginning to feel like some sort of weird dream. And the same as in a dream, she didn't know what to say or do. Her whole world seemed eerily suspended.

Tina leaned across the table.

"You haven't changed, not one bit," Tina said. "You like to have friends over to visit. You like to ride your bike. You like music. And you were always so trusting of the people around you. I've changed, though. I guess I shouldn't be surprised that you don't know me."

Tina's voice had shifted from a higher pitch to a hollow baritone. She lifted her hand up to the side of her head and tugged at her hair and...

A wig! Joyce realized.

The wig fell away, and Joyce saw that the person sitting across the table from her was a man. She recognized him from the photo the agents had shown her, and also from her walks in the neighborhood.

It's him.

It's the killer.

Her whole body was flooded with panic now. She wanted to scream or jump up from her chair and rush out of the room. But she felt mute and paralyzed. She couldn't move or make the slightest sound. She couldn't even breathe.

The man said, "Soon you'll understand. Soon you'll know who both of us are."

With a blinding, snakelike movement, he was out of his chair and had grabbed her by the hair. Seemingly out of nowhere, he now had a knife in his hand. He pulled her head back, and Joyce could feel that he was about to slam her head against the table.

But Joyce's paralysis suddenly vanished. With a huge gasp of air, she pushed violently against him, feeling hair rip out of her scalp as he tumbled away. She started to dart to the door. But again he moved with uncanny swiftness, standing square in front of the door blocking her way.

He was smiling sadly now.

"Please don't do this, Rachel," he said. "Just let me take care of everything. This doesn't have to be hard. It doesn't even have to hurt."

She tried to charge past him toward the door, but he grabbed her by the hair again.

This time he managed to slam her head against the wall.

Joyce struggled against the dizziness that threatened to overwhelm her.

CHAPTER THIRTY ONE

Riley was in her hotel bathroom trying to scrub the stench of garbage off her hands. The cell phone they'd dug out of the dumpster had left smelly traces behind, and though the odor was slight, it troubled her. She didn't envy poor Officer Ornstein, who'd had to climb all the way into the dumpster to find the damned thing.

It'll be days before he gets rid of the smell, she thought.

Finally Riley decided that the hotel soap had sufficiently overcome the odor of garbage and she turned off the faucet. She needed to go next door to thoroughly debrief the young woman she and Bill had brought in for protection. They'd put Joyce Rowland in the same adjoining room that Jenn had occupied before she'd taken off.

Riley dried her hands and stepped out of the bathroom.

She heard a violent crash in the next room.

What could be going on in there?

She dashed to the doors that separated the two rooms. She pulled her own door open, but the other was locked. She pounded hard on the door, but no one answered, and the racket on the other side only continued.

Finally, she threw herself violently against the door, breaking it open. As she staggered into the room, she could hardly believe the sight that met her eyes.

There he was—the killer himself, weirdly clad in what seemed to be women's clothes.

The woman was on her knees on the floor, and he was bent over her, gripping her by the hair.

He was holding a knife to her throat.

The woman whimpered and looked dazed, and Riley could see a bruise on her forehead. She realized the killer must have just now knocked Joyce nearly unconscious.

Riley froze in place. She didn't dare charge at him. She couldn't even draw her gun.

He was one swift move away from fatally slicing the young woman's throat.

He stared straight at Riley with wild, crazed eyes, but he slowly straightened up.

"Aunt Heather!" he murmured.

Riley was briefly startled to hear him call her by that name. Then she remembered the family picture in the killer's apartment, and the woman both she and Bill had noticed bore a marked resemblance to her.

He thinks I'm her, Riley realized.

In fact, he'd probably targeted her all along. She knew her face was all over the local news right now. He'd probably seen her on TV.

Riley took a few deep breaths.

Now she knew exactly what she had to do.

Austin Crane tried to fight down his shock at seeing that face. He had no reason to be surprised, after all. He'd known she was just in the next room. He'd planned to go there and take her soul as soon as he was finished with Rachel. But now here they were, both in the same room at the same time. He hadn't expected anything like this.

Aunt Heather shook her head and said to him …

"Austin, what are you doing to your sister?"

The knife shook slightly in his hands. Aunt Heather seemed to be in one of her sterner moods. And it was small wonder. She could obviously see how much of a mess he was making of something that ought to be so simple.

"Just let me finish this, Aunt Heather," Austin said. "I'm sorry for how this looks. I'll get it done, I promise. All I want is for all of us to be together again."

"I understand that," Aunt Heather said. "But…"

She paused for a moment. Then a look of sadness crossed her face.

She said, "But why do I have to be last?"

Austin felt stricken with guilt now. The last thing he had wanted to do was hurt Aunt Heather's feelings. But that was exactly what he'd done.

Again, he thought he heard Mom's voice calling out to him.

"Austin! Dinner's ready!"

He felt a knot of sadness in his throat as he remembered ignoring that call.

Poor Aunt Heather!

She'd made a special trip to be with the family for dinner that evening.

How hurt she must have been when he ignored his mother's call!

As if I didn't want to see her.

As if I didn't want to have dinner with her.

He felt a single sob burst out of his throat.

"I'm sorry, Aunt Heather," he said. "You know I love you, don't you?"

Aunt Heather shook her head.

"I'm not sure I do," she said. "Not anymore. At least you don't love me as much as you do the others."

She took a step toward him.

"Can't I please be next? Why do I have to be the last? The very last?"

She took a slow step toward him.

"Take me first," she said, touching her throat gently. "I want this so badly. I've wanted it for such a long time."

Austin nodded, then pushed Rachel's almost limp body out of the way.

Holding his knife out, he stepped forward to meet Aunt Heather.
She seized him by the wrist.

Shocked, he managed to wrench himself free, and he began to understand that he'd been wrong about Aunt Heather.

Carrying his go-bag, Bill stepped out of the elevator onto the third floor. His mind was buzzing with thoughts about the unfinished case, and he was anxious to talk to Riley about how they should proceed.

He glanced down the hall and noticed something odd.

Where is Agent Barnes?

He'd expected the local field agent to be standing outside the room where they'd brought Joyce Rowland for protection.

Nothing to worry about, Bill thought. *Barnes is probably inside talking with her.*

He was thirsty, and it occurred to him that it might be nice to have soft drinks when he sat down to talk with Riley, so he headed for the nearby nook that held vending machines.

He staggered backward at what he saw there.

One of the vending machines was splattered with blood, and there was even more on the floor, trailing toward a door marked EMPLOYEES ONLY.

Bill opened the door and gasped.

Agent Barnes's dead body was lying there in a pool of blood, his eyes still wide open.

She's not Aunt Heather anymore, Austin thought with alarm.

Instead, she really was FBI Agent Riley Paige.

And she was extremely strong and agile.

She had knocked the knife out of his hand, and he didn't know where it fell. Then she lunged at him, and he picked up a chair to fend her off. He waved it desperately to keep her away from him.

Through the din of their struggle, he heard a loud repeated noise.

Someone's pounding on the door.

He quickly realized it must be another agent—most likely the male partner he'd seen her with earlier.

I can't fight them both, he thought.

Austin threw the chair at Agent Paige, then turned and ran through the door that separated the two rooms.

He dashed toward the exit door of the other room.

Bill could hear some kind of struggle going on inside the room where the woman was being kept.

He was about to draw his service weapon and shoot the door latch off when he caught a movement in his peripheral vision. He turned in time to see the door to Riley's room fly open. Someone dressed in what looked like a woman's pantsuit rushed out into the hall,

With remarkable swiftness and agility, the figure dashed past him and darted down a stairwell.

Bill recognized that face in an instant.

Austin Crane.

Bill broke into a run after him.

He stormed down the stairs and caught up with his prey on the last flight of steps. Bill tackled the younger man, and they both rolled down the remaining steps into the hotel lobby, where they lay in a tangled heap together.

Bill pulled himself loose from Austin Crane, who staggered to his feet and looked as though he might run again.

Bill pulled his service weapon and pointed it straight at Crane.

"Don't move," he commanded.

Crane wavered in indecision.

"I'll shoot you if I have to," Bill told him.

Crane's expression drooped with despair and he stood perfectly still.

An alert hotel security man came over to help Bill take him into custody. As Bill put his gun back in his holster, he realized he'd really meant those words he'd just said.

"I'll shoot."

Bill smiled as he put Crane in handcuffs.

He knew his struggle with PTSD was over. He'd killed the last criminal because he'd had to, and he would have shot this one too.

I'm back in the game, he thought.

CHAPTER THIRTY TWO

Riley suppressed a groan as she lay back on her hotel bed and continued talking on her cell phone. She ached all over and she was certain she was going to hurt for days after her desperate struggle with Austin Crane. She was sure that Bill was in even worse shape from his wild tumble down a flight of stairs while grappling with Austin Crane. Fortunately, neither of them had been seriously injured.

Despite her pain, Riley was feeling very happy.

Gabriela's Spanish-accented voice over the phone was giving her encouraging news.

"I wish you could have caught the girls before they left," Gabriela was saying. "April is playing soccer this afternoon, and Jilly has gone to cheer for her."

"Oh, yes, I remember," Riley said. "It's a big game, isn't it?"

"*Sí*, very big. And April is confident that her school will win."

"I hope so," Riley said. "It sure sounds like the girls are getting along better."

"They are," Gabriela assured her. "They're through fighting, thank goodness, at least for now. The teen years are very difficult, so of course it is to be expected. They will get through this time, they always do."

"I hope so," Riley said.

Although sometimes I wonder, she thought.

Riley couldn't seem to shake off her bitterness at April's terrible lapse of responsibility with the gun.

Gabriela asked, "When will you be coming home?"

"Well, since Bill and I have solved the case, it looks like we'll be flying back tonight," Riley said. "We'll have to debrief in Quantico, but then I can come straight home."

"I'll have something good ready to eat," Gabriela said.

Riley almost said, *"Please, you needn't bother."*

But she quickly thought better of it. Once Gabriela had her mind set on fixing one of her Guatemalan specialties, there was no talking her out of it. Besides, it would be nice to have a lovely meal to look forward to tonight.

She and Gabriela ended the call, and Riley lay there thinking how it would feel to be home again.

Would it feel nice?

Or would it just feel strange?

Sometimes it could be jarring to go home after hunting down a dangerous killer. Riley could never help feeling as though she were bringing some of that evil home with her. And the evil she'd struggled with this time was especially troubling. Austin Crane had been truly insane—one of those killers she sometimes faced who really harbored no malice toward his victims. To her, that was the strangest kind of killer she could imagine.

She shuddered as she remembered her glimpses into his troubled mind.

Put it behind you, she told herself.

But it was hard to shake off her feelings about this case. Things had turned out so differently than she'd hoped. She'd had no idea that the killer's last victim would be an FBI agent. She hated to think of what a blow this was going to be to Agent Barnes's family and other loved ones.

As she tried to shift her thoughts back to home and what she might do with the kids tomorrow, there was a knock at the door.

She rose slowly to her feet and went to the door. In the hallway stood a hotel employee holding sturdy, shoebox-sized box.

"I've got a delivery for you, ma'am," he said.

Riley was puzzled. Who did she even know who had any idea that she'd be in this hotel?

"Are you sure?" Riley asked.

"Is your name Riley Paige?" the man asked.

"Yes," Riley said.

"Then this is definitely for you. It was brought by a delivery service."

Riley's heart sank as she saw the return address. The package was from Jenn Roston, and it had been sent from Dallas, Texas.

Riley signed for the package and took it back into her room. She set it down on the table and opened it. She gasped at what she found inside. Wrapped up in bubble wrap were Jenn's badge and her gun.

She remembered what Chief Meredith had said to her over the phone.

"I've got a resignation letter, but what I don't have are a badge and a gun. She wouldn't have happened to leave those with you, would she?"

Now Riley had both of those items—plus another two-word note that said...

I tried.

Riley understood perfectly. With this package, Jenn was wrapping up her final business with the FBI.

Riley burst into tears, swept by a flood of bitterness toward her one-time friend. She knew exactly what this meant. Jenn had returned once and for all to the dark world of her childhood—to the world of Aunt Cora. Jenn had turned her back on Riley once and for all.

"Why?" Riley sobbed aloud, wiping her face with a tissue.

Why did people keep betraying her trust like this? Ryan had broken his marriage vows over and over again before he was gone for good. She'd had hopes that things would be better with Blaine, but now those hopes were crushed.

Could she ever really trust anyone at all?

Her whole life seemed to tell her otherwise. Even her own father hadn't been a source of stability for her. She'd never known what to expect from him—whether he was going to help her or hurt her.

Was she doomed to be hurt by everyone she cared about?

As if in reply, there came another knock at the door. Riley smiled through her tears.

She knew that gentle but firm knock well. It was as distinctive and individual as a fingerprint.

It's Bill.

She went to the door and opened it. Bill's mouth dropped open as he saw Riley's face.

"Hey, what's the matter?" he said.

Riley realized that she hadn't wiped away the tears. She mutely showed Bill the box with the badge and the gun. She could tell by his sympathetic expression that he immediately understood what this meant.

Someday maybe I'll tell him the whole truth about Jenn, she thought. *He deserves it.*

They sat down on the bed together, and Bill held Riley's hand comfortingly.

Riley shook her head and said, "And on top of everything else, I've just finished my last case ever. I still haven't decided whether to resign or let Meredith go ahead and fire me."

Bill scoffed and said, "Meredith's not going to fire you. I could tell when I talked to him. He was worried sick about you. He knew something was really wrong. Don't you know that he thinks of you like a daughter?"

Riley gasped at Bill's words. She had never imagined such a thing. But she suddenly felt certain that Bill was telling her the truth. Meredith would surely give her a reprimand, and she didn't doubt that she deserved it. But he wasn't going to let her go.

Then she laughed through her tears and said, "So—how are *you* feeling?"

Bill laughed as well. Then his expression grew serious.

"I'm not sure I'm feeling a whole lot better than you are," he said.

"Really?" Riley said. "Why not?"

Bill said haltingly, "Well, it's kind of hard to explain, but…"

Bill gripped Riley's hand more tightly, and his voice choked as he spoke.

"Riley, you were a target again. Another madman wanted to kill *you*."

Riley smiled and touched his face. Trying to make light of things, she said, "It's nothing, Bill. Lots of people have wanted to kill me over the years. And lots of times with pretty good reason, I suspect."

But Bill's expression looked rather hurt now, and she knew she shouldn't have said that.

"Riley, listen to me," Bill said. "I don't think I could stand to ever lose you. I don't think I could live without you."

Riley looked into his eyes.

She wanted to tell him she understood, that she felt the same way about him.

But somehow, any words seemed perfectly unnecessary. She could feel that they were both losing themselves in their shared gazes. Then neither their jobs nor any other responsibilities could stand between them.

At long last, their lips met.

Now Available for Pre-Order!

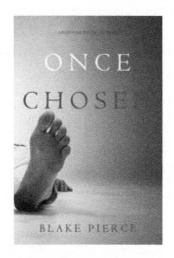

ONCE CHOSEN
(A Riley Paige Mystery—Book 17)

"A masterpiece of thriller and mystery! The author did a magnificent job developing characters with a psychological side that is so well described that we feel inside their minds, follow their fears and cheer for their success. The plot is very intelligent and will keep you entertained throughout the book. Full of twists, this book will keep you awake until the turn of the last page."
—Books and Movie Reviews, Roberto Mattos (re Once Gone)

ONCE CHOSEN is book #17 in the bestselling Riley Paige mystery series, which begins with the #1 bestseller ONCE GONE (Book #1)—a free download with over 1,000 five star reviews!

A serial killer strikes every Halloween—the bodies of his victims re-surfacing years later—and with Halloween only days away, it is up to FBI Special Agent Riley Paige to stop the killer before he strikes again.

How has this killer gone undetected for so long? How many victims have there really been? And who will he target next?

FBI Special Agent Riley Paige must fend off her own demons and her dysfunctional family life as she races against time to enter the mind of a diabolical killer days away from striking again—one who may even be more brilliant than her.

Can she stop him in time?

An action-packed psychological suspense thriller with heart-pounding suspense, ONCE CHOSEN is book #17 in a riveting series—with a beloved character—that will leave you turning pages late into the night.

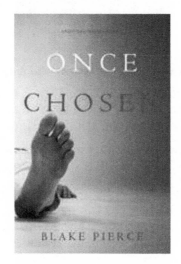

ONCE CHOSEN
(A Riley Paige Mystery—Book 17)

Did you know that I've written multiple novels in the mystery genre? If you haven't read all my series, click the image below to download a series starter!

Made in the USA
Monee, IL
27 May 2022

97141699R00142